Vexed in Venice

A Lucy Tuppence Mystery

MONICA KNIGHTLEY

ISBN-13: 978-1717387172
ISBN-10: 1717387179

Also by Monica Knightley

The Stratford Upon Avondale Mysteries:
ALAS, SHE DROWNED
COME, BITTER POISON
O HAPPY DAGGER
'TIS THE WITCHING TIME
HITHER TO LONDON
THE LADY DOTH PROTEST
MUCH ADO

Paranormal Romances from Soul Mate Publishing:

THE VAMPIRE'S PASSION
MISS AUSTEN'S VAMPIRE

Writing as Monica Duddington:

BAND GEEKS AND RIPTIDES
(a Young Adult contemporary novel from
Soul Mate Publishing)

To Ken Rimany, who, as we strolled around the charming island of Burano, shared with me an idea for a perfect Venetian murder.

⌒ one ⌒

LUCY TUPPENCE COULD ONLY WONDER if there wasn't a law on the books in some country, any country, against what her lifelong dear friend, and now employer, Hester Nilsson was requiring of her at that moment. She glanced over at her fellow employees and friends, Carrie Silva and Oscar Kapoor, who were also huffing and puffing and appeared to be on the verge of collapse.

After all, they had just arrived after spending nearly twenty-four hours in the air and in hub airports.

"You will thank me when you awake refreshed and on the local time zone tomorrow morning," Hester trilled over her shoulder to her three wheezing friends as they trudged up the stairs of the Rialto Bridge over Venice's Grand Canal. "This glorious sunshine and exercise will do the trick, I promise you."

Lucy entertained a fantasy of throwing the tall, blond beauty into the canal, far below.

"We get that," Carrie groaned as they reached the top of

the bridge. "It's just that this amazing city is basically the world's Stairmaster, what with all these bridges every ten feet. And Hester, we're tired." Carrie wasn't one for complaining, but Lucy was happy to accept her assistance in this matter.

"I know we're tired," Hester said as she paused at the top of the bridge to take in the view. "But you'll be happy you did this when we have to get going to Burano first thing tomorrow morning. Our boat will be leaving San Marco at nine o'clock. Sharp."

Lucy welcomed the pause. Her breath caught in her throat at the sight before her eyes. The sun threw diamonds upon the water of the canal, which was being navigated by so many water taxis, vaporetti, and sleek, graceful gondolas Lucy was surprised none of them were running into one another. And the sight of the massive, Byzantine *palazzi,* or palatial buildings, that lined the canal made her feel like she'd just fallen back in time to the sixteenth century.

Her white linen capris and navy poly-blend blouse felt out of place—or rather, time.

As she enjoyed the sun on her face, it occurred to her that Venice is a place of light and shadow. Shadow in the narrow *calli*, or alleys, that form a labyrinth of passages across the island and where light must fight to reach; and light out on the water, and reflected off the small canals, and in the little squares that they'd just marched through. And here on the Rialto Bridge, it was all brilliant light.

Hester stepped up next to where Lucy stood leaning on the railing and put an arm around her friend's back. "I can't believe this is actually happening. All those months of planning, and here we are." Lucy smiled at Hester and wondered what Hester had eaten that had left that green smudge on her upper lip.

"Boss," Oscar said, as he too leaned on the railing gawking at the stunning view. "You want me to take some pictures from up here? The angle of the light right now would be perfect for some stunning photos for the magazine."

While the three women had been able to leave all of their luggage at the hotel, Oscar had chosen to bring his still camera and a case of lenses. The quintessential American son of Indian immigrants, Oscar didn't share his family's stunning good looks. A pinched face, large buckteeth, and thick glasses that made his eyes appear huge gave him the look of a nutty Jim Carrey character. His quick wit and sharp intelligence had a tendency to surprise people when they first met him.

Hester turned to him. "I've told you not to call me that, Oscar. We are all equals here in this new venture. One for all and all for one, and all that."

He shrugged. "It's just that you're the money, Hester, which in my book makes you the boss. But if you don't like it, I'll refrain from using that term." Oscar bowed with a dramatic flourish.

"Nilsson European Adventures is the four of us," she said, not only to Oscar but Lucy and Carrie as well. "We each have our jobs, which play to our individual talents, and without any one of us, there would be no Nilsson European

Adventures. And sure, please do take some pictures. That's an excellent idea."

Having known Hester her entire life, Lucy acknowledged the fact that Hester could easily annoy her, but she also had a good deal of admiration for the woman. When Hester had inherited her late parents' billions of dollars, she didn't start living the life of a pampered princess. Instead, she set up a foundation that currently was improving the lives of people all over the world, kept her parents' high-tech business going with the help of a trusted CEO and staff, and continued to work on her research in microbiology. Biology was only one of the three master's degrees she earned at Oxford back when she turned down the seven-figure modeling career with a top New York agency.

So it was no surprise that when she gathered her four best, and oldest friends from childhood and told them her idea for the travel magazine and its associated website and YouTube channel, all of them were quickly on board.

They all trusted the woman. And they each had reasons for desiring a change in their lives.

However, Hester's ideas of how to deal with jet lag left something to be desired in Lucy's estimation.

Carrie fanned herself. "Hester, I appreciate everything you're saying, but as the in-front-of-camera talent I'm just saying I need my beauty sleep before I get in front of that camera tomorrow and talk about lace-making on Burano," Carrie said, referring to the Venetian island renowned for its lace.

Hester smiled warmly at her friend. "And you will get that beauty sleep, I promise."

The other three friends often referred to Carrie as their own walking United Nations. Her DNA represented five of the seven continents, and her features were a map to all of those exotic places. Her light brown complexion was sprinkled with freckles. Her brown eyes were almost as dark as Oscar's, and her hair was naturally a light brown. But the color changed with Carrie's whims. On this day a green streak accented one side of her head. A tribute to Italy and her flag, she'd told them. At five foot four she was the same height as Lucy, but curvier. Carrie liked to refer to herself as voluptuous.

"Now I have a surprise for you grumpy grumps," Hester said cheerily, as she started down the stairs that led to the other side of the canal.

Lucy exchanged a look with Carrie, who rolled her eyes.

The bridge was packed with tourists traveling both ways over the span and the group couldn't stay together as they were bumped and jostled by the throngs. As Lucy fought her way down the steps, she heard multiple languages spoken. She marveled at how people from every corner of the globe flocked to the beautiful Venice. Looking over the heads surrounding her, she took in the scene beyond the bridge and understood why.

Continuing down the stairs, Lucy found herself at the rear of their foursome.

Perhaps it was the fatigue, but Lucy wondered, as she kept her group in sight, if she hadn't aged as well as her three friends. All of them were forty-five now, but Lucy knew she had more lines on her face and had been coloring her graying brown hair for years. She had been fighting a losing battle with the same fifteen pounds for longer than she wished to admit. And her newly acquired hairstyle of a casual flip above her shoulders had given her a brief feeling of renewed youth, but the feeling hadn't lasted long. As Lucy tucked a strand of hair behind her ear, she cursed what the hours on the planes had done to her new style.

This new adventure was to be the tonic she badly needed. And while Venice was the most gloriously beautiful place she'd ever been to, she silently wondered if she was up to what her adventure was going to require of her.

At the bottom of the bridge, Lucy could see five foot ten inch Hester in the distance, standing next to the canal.

She joined her friends who were standing expectantly in front of the grinning Hester. So close to the water, Lucy could smell the familiar salty, slightly fishy scent she was accustomed to back home in California's Bay Area. It smelled like a San Francisco wharf. Yet, here there was something exotic that had been added to the mix.

Hester threw her arms out to her sides, and said, "Ta-da! We're going on a gondola ride!"

All of the sweat and pain and anxieties melted away from Lucy as she grinned back at Hester.

A gondola ride in Venice, Italy.

Truly, *la dolce vita* couldn't get much better than that.

As it turned out, *la dolce vita* could get better.

After they got settled onto the long, black, shiny,

straight-from-a-fantasy gondola, they were joined by two men who sat at the very front of the boat.

One carried an accordion.

The other carried an aura about him that made Lucy's toes wiggle in her walking sneakers. She tried not to stare at him but found herself stealing glances at his handsome Italian face as the gondolier in his traditional black and white striped shirt stood at the back of the boat and navigated his way away from the dock and into the multitude of boats on the Grand Canal.

Once on the canal, the accordion player began playing a familiar tune. Lucy couldn't immediately place it but knew it was a classic Italian song.

The handsome man stood, placed one hand on his chest, and in a spectacular operatic voice began singing.

Tears wasted no time popping up in Lucy's eyes.

Her face beamed as she sat riveted to the sound of the man's voice.

As the water lapped at the sides of the gondola, and the warm May sun caressed her face, Lucy briefly wondered if she had died and gone to heaven. After the hell of the past two years, the idea of heaven had seemed impossible.

Their gondolier expertly made his way through the many boats which came at them from every direction. Normally, Lucy would have worried about the safety of the operation, but so entranced by the music and singing, she paid no heed to the canal traffic.

Just as the gondolier took them into one of the romantic small, narrow canals that crisscross all of Venice, the singer came to the end of the song, and without more than a beat or two of silence the accordion began playing again. This time there was no mistaking the song—Santa Lucia. Maybe a little cheesy, but it sent a shiver down Lucy's spine, nonetheless.

Within the canyon made by the ancient buildings that rose up from the sides of the canal, the sound of the singer's voice became richer.

Without realizing what she was doing, Lucy began to sing along, the foreign words tripping off her tongue as if Italian were her native language.

The opera singer smiled broadly at Lucy, which encouraged her to sing in a full voice. As an occasional vocalist for a rock band, her voice was accustomed to filling all of the available space.

As the gondola approached a bridge the dozen or so people crossing it stopped to watch and listen to the duet. Every one of them smiled ear to ear at the Venetian charm they were unexpectedly treated to.

The gondolier artfully moved the gondola under the short bridge, and as he did so both he and the singer ducked down. When they came out on the other side, their impromptu audience scurried to the other side of the bridge to catch more of the performance.

The boat hadn't moved far beyond the bridge when the two singers hit the last dramatic notes of the song, and the bridge audience clapped and shouted "Bravo!"

With his eyes on Lucy, the singer sat down and leaned toward her. "You have a beautiful voice, Signora." Lucy's cheeks warmed for the first time in years. She estimated the man to be in his early fifties, his full head of wavy hair still a dark brown with only a few wisps of gray at his temples. Heavy-lidded dark eyes smiled at her from a face chiseled from one of the ancient Roman statues.

Lucy tugged at the hem of her blouse. "Thank you, uh, *grazie*. You certainly are gifted with a wonderful voice, Signor."

The singer lowered his head in a show of humility and thanked her.

"My name is Nicolo. Nicolo Gavelli." He held out his hand, and Lucy took it and gave it a gentle shake. His grip was strong.

Lucy introduced herself and her friends.

Speaking to all of them, but focusing more on Lucy, Nicolo said, "You must come see me at La Fenice. I'm performing in *Rigoletto* for this week and next."

"La Fenice is the opera house, right?" Lucy asked.

"It is. It is a beautiful opera house, glorious. You must see it, Lucy." He smiled at her in a way that made her blush again. Then he quickly added, waving at the group on the boat, "You all must see Teatro La Fenice. A treasure in Venice."

"Actually…" Carrie said, "We do plan to visit and take pictures. We're travel writers and researchers and will be visiting it in just a few days."

"And seeing an opera would be quite a treat," Hester added.

"I will get you tickets!" Nicolo cheered.

A date was chosen, and Nicolo stood again.

"Miss Lucy, do you have a request for another duet?"

"Oh my…yes…uh, how about Ave Maria?"

Nicolo patted his chest and closed his eyes. "My favorite. Yes."

The accordion player struck the first notes and Nicolo and Lucy entranced everyone within hearing distance with their rendition of the classic song.

By the end, Lucy's eyes were filled with tears, and when she glanced at Hester and Carrie, she saw tears running down their cheeks.

Yes, this is la dolce vita, Lucy thought. *No more sitting in a cubicle analyzing crime data. No more dealing with my divorce negotiations, and ending an old life. This new life might just be the answer to my prayers.*

~ two ~

THE NEWLY MINTED TRAVEL WRITERS, researchers, and photographer gaped at the brightly colored buildings that surrounded the *piazza* at the heart of Burano. Houses and shops that came in all shades of pinks, oranges, greens, purples, and blues made it impossible not to experience a feeling none of the four friends, and now co-workers, had felt in the several years prior to coming to Venice.

Joy.

A childlike joy.

Lucy had known little, if any, joy working crime analysis in an office cubicle in San Francisco. Carrie hadn't been given many opportunities for joyful experiences working as a translator in the American Embassy in Lisbon, Portugal while her second marriage fell apart. Lucy knew that Oscar had been wasting his talents producing corporate videos for a small studio in New York, a job that surely didn't bring much joy or satisfaction to his life. And Hester, normally a person who sought out life's joys, had gone through a difficult two years following the deaths of her parents.

But now, here they were in a foreign city that's very existence brings delight to anyone fortunate enough to visit it.

Though she'd be loath to admit it, Lucy was thankful that Hester had put them through their death march across Venice the day before. She woke refreshed and humming tunes from the gondola ride. The brightly colored sundress she wore matched her mood.

She was amused to see that Carrie had also dressed in a colorful sundress, while Hester wore a simple pale yellow sheath dress. Oscar, despite their admonitions about men wearing shorts in Europe, was wearing cargo shorts and a polo shirt.

Multiple cafes along the square added to the ambience with their aromas of coffee, herbs, spices, and seafood, which wafted through the island air.

Though it was still only ten in the morning, the *piazza* was filled with tourists enjoying a day of food and shopping on the candy box island. Travelers gawked and pointed and chatted loudly as they moved through the square.

There wasn't a grumpy person to be found on Burano.

It had been a short walk from the boat landing to the Museo del Merletto, the lace museum. Burano is famous for its lace.

"Closed?" Carrie shouted, staring at the sign written in three languages: Italian, English, and another that looked vaguely Italian. "Are you kidding me? You said the website said they were open on Tuesdays." She glared at Lucy, who was in charge of logistics and the research necessary to form those plans.

"What can I say?" Lucy replied to her overwrought friend. "It said they'd be open. See the sign, it says it's a bank holiday." Lucy became aware that her tone had taken on an ugly edge, and forced herself to dial it back. "I guess the webmaster didn't think to make a note of that on the site."

"What's that third language?" Oscar interjected.

"The Venetian dialect," Hester told them. "Though Mussolini made Italian the country's official language, some of the older people in each of the old republics still hold on to their dialects."

Lucy shot a look at her friend and gave her head a little shake of disbelief, despite knowing that Hester had always been the keeper of all trivia. Her brain worked like a computer and could pull up the most arcane bits of information in mere seconds.

"Huh, I never knew that," Carrie said. "Thanks, Hester. But it still messes up our plans!"

Oscar placed a hand on Carrie's shoulder. "Your temper is ruining the zen of this place. Hey, we're in Italy, go with the flow." One hand made gentle waving motions, like the water taxi on the *laguna* that they had taken to this island. "I don't know about you, Carrie, but this gig is so exceedingly better than what I've been doing for the past few years, I can't think of a reason to complain about anything. I'm simply going to enjoy the ride."

After gracing Oscar with a broad smile, Hester focused her eyes on Lucy. "Lucy, what do you suggest as a backup plan?"

Lucy squared her shoulders. "My research indicates that there are plenty of lace shops on the island and that some of those have women making lace in them. Tourists are welcome to watch."

"Good," Carrie chirped. "Maybe Oscar should start with the B-roll footage of the square and the shops and cafes. While he's doing that we can look for one of those places with lacemakers."

With a new plan in place, the three women left Oscar to get his camera ready and start filming, while they joined the flow of tourists walking through the *piazza*.

They strolled through the square, which eventually lengthened out—becoming more of a pedestrian street, passing nothing but cafes and shops selling goods made of lace. Every shop had large displays set up outside of their establishment. Most of the lace shops sold items that looked much more machine-made than handmade with inexpensive prices to go along with the cheap souvenirs.

Lucy noticed a shop with what looked like the real deal—small, delicate lace items such as doilies and napkins were on display outside. She picked up her pace, eager to speak to the shopkeeper who stood with her goods.

"*Buongiorno*," she greeted the tall, slender, middle-aged Venetian woman.

"Hello," she replied in clear English. Lucy felt slightly deflated that she'd been so easily pegged as an American.

"Your lace is beautiful," Lucy said as she ran a finger over a doily. "I was hoping to see lace being made, but the museum is closed today. Do you happen to have anyone here making lace?"

"I am so sorry. We do not. However, the shop two doors down has someone making lace today. Perhaps you would like to purchase that doily? It was made right here by my mother."

"I might," Lucy lied. "I'll be back after I find the lacemaker. Thank you so much for the help. *Grazie.*"

She hurried into the street and caught up to Hester and Carrie.

"That blue shop, right there," Lucy said, pointing, "is supposed to have a lace maker."

The three women made their way to the shop. A sandwich board stood in front of the shop. *Lacemaking today.*

The shopkeeper stood in the doorway. She was older and significantly shorter than the other shopkeeper. The woman wore a simple blue cotton dress that was topped off with a scarf with lacing at its edges. Lucy told her they hoped to see lacemaking.

"Oh yes, yes." The woman bobbed her head several times. "Up the stairs. Aurelia is making lace. Go right along."

"Grazie," the three friends said in turn as they entered the shop. They had to make their way through narrow aisles stuffed with everything from table linens to wall hangings, before they found the staircase.

They began climbing the stairs, and the shopkeeper joined them, bringing up the rear. As she climbed, she called out, "Aurelia. Aurelia." Lucy guessed this was Aurelia's warning to stop reading an Italian celebrity magazine or playing a game on her phone and get to the lace making.

Once at the top of the stairs they found themselves in a small, crowded space. A comfortable armchair sat in the center, surrounded by stacks of fabric and lace and spools of thread. Everything one needed to make lace goods.

Except for a lacemaker.

"Aurelia?" The shopkeeper's voice went up an octave. "Aurelia?"

The area was so small there was no place for the missing woman to be hiding.

Then, turning to the potential customers, she said, "I don't know where she could be. She should be right here."

Lucy forced a polite smile. "Maybe we can come back in a little while. Do you think she might be here later?"

"Oh, yes. Yes, yes. She will be here." To Lucy's ears, the words sounded more hopeful than confident.

Hester addressed the woman, in perfect Italian. The shopkeeper beamed. Then, in English, she added, "We will be back."

Outside, Carrie asked Hester what she'd said.

"I told her I'd be back to buy a tablecloth I had my eye on."

"Do you know how much that will cost?" Carrie asked in a squeal. "I saw those prices. Eight hundred euros for one of those tablecloths!"

Lucy laughed and nudged Carrie. "Really? You're worried our billionaire friend can't afford that?"

"Touché," she said with a rueful laugh.

"You're talking about me like I'm not here again," Hester said softly.

Hester was the only child of brilliant visionaries whose educational grounding in electrical engineering allowed the high-tech innovations they created—innovations that changed the way people lived. The Nilssons also helped put the Silicon Valley on the map. They had both died two years earlier, leaving their empire and legacy to their equally brilliant daughter.

The three women came to a canal that divided the street into two sides and began to cross its Venetian style bridge when a sharp scream rent the air.

A knot of people gathered next to the canal not fifty feet down from the bridge.

Lucy, who had spent nearly two decades working for a police department, albeit in a civilian role, didn't hesitate a second before breaking into a run down the steps and along the canal to the growing group of people.

She pushed her way to the canal side.

Around her, people whimpered and cried as their eyes were riveted to the sight in the water.

Just below the surface of the water and close to the edge of the canal floated the body of a woman, face down.

Around her neck, a length of lace was knotted. Factory-made lace.

Somewhere behind Lucy, a man screamed, "Aurelia!"

It appeared they had found their missing lacemaker.

~ three ~

LUCY SIPPED THE ESPRESSO THAT Aurelia's employer, Signora Di Votti, insisted she drink, claiming Lucy had experienced a shock. She sat in a backroom of the shop, along with Hester, Carrie, and Oscar. The room was stacked from floor to ceiling with wares just waiting to find a place in the front shop.

It had been an hour since Aurelia's body was discovered, and Signora Di Votti had been wiping tears from her face since she first heard the news. The wait for the police to come talk to them was growing tedious. An officer, dressed in a military uniform and who had been well-armed, had been adamant that they wait at the shop—he wanted to speak with Lucy and Signora Di Votti.

"Aurelia. She was like a *figlia*, a daughter, to me. Always so…kind…" A sob interrupted the Signora's thoughts. Shaking her head, while mopping tears with a handkerchief that looked like it had been made on the premises, she excused herself and exited through the back door. From where she sat, Lucy could see through the doorway to a *calle*—or narrow pedestrian street—and the house on the other side of it.

Lucy swallowed the rest of the small cup of the elixir and made a humphing sound.

"I'm not sure I trust the Carabinieri to handle this," Lucy proclaimed to her friends.

"Who? What?" Carrie asked, her mouth hanging open.

"They're a type of Italian military police. We saw some yesterday in the Piazza San Marco, remember?" Hester explained, dipping into her font of knowledge. "They had the red berets and big machine guns…" From the looks on Oscar and Carrie's faces, they remembered all too well. There was nothing like enjoying an evening cocktail in a magnificent historical square and watching heavily armed military weaving their way through the crowds.

"Yeah," Lucy concurred. "On our way from the dock I happened to notice that they have an office right near the docks, so they were the first to arrive. But I don't think they investigate murders. I think that's handled by the state police in the area. I'm guessing they're headquartered in Venice proper."

"And we care about this…why?" Oscar asked, his eyes narrowed behind the thick glasses.

Lucy felt all eyes focus on her.

"Well…" Lucy said, drawing out the word, stalling for time. The truth was she wasn't entirely sure why she cared. But she did. Strongly.

"I suppose it's because I saw her body there in the canal. So soon after we were looking for her. I feel…I feel a responsibility to her."

"Might we remind you that you no longer work in the world of law enforcement," Oscar said.

"I can understand how you feel," Hester said, coming to her defense. "It had to be a shock."

Lucy reached over to Hester and squeezed her hand. "Thank you, Hester," she said while shooting an icy glare at Oscar.

A silence fell over the group before Lucy added, "I think we should see what information we can get about Aurelia before the police get here. We should be talking to Signora Di Votti. Now." She stood up and made her way to the outer door.

Like ducklings following their mother, the other three got up and followed Lucy, but not without moans and a muffled expletive or two.

They found the grieving shop owner leaning against the bright blue wall of the building, smoking a cigarette.

"Signora, we are sorry to interrupt your private time," Lucy said. "But we were hoping you could tell us a little about your friend, Aurelia. We feel saddened we didn't get to know her." Lucy could almost hear Oscar saying, "speak for yourself." But she knew a display of empathy was the only way to get the information she wanted.

The woman shifted her gaze from one to the other of the little group, making significant eye contact with each. "That is kind of you. I would be happy to tell you about Aurelia."

"Was she married?" Hester asked.

Signora Di Votti tipped her head back and forth. "Yes, and no. She was separated from her husband. He is a, how you say, difficult man. Gets angry. Especially when drinking, you know?"

They all nodded, waiting for her to continue.

"Aurelia is…was…lucky though. She had the family home after her mother died, so she went there to live when she left the husband."

Lucy wanted desperately to take her notebook out and start writing everything down, but knew that wouldn't be appropriate. She hoped that between the four of them they could remember everything they heard. Surely, Hester, the keeper of all trivia and minutiae, would recall the finer details.

"That is very fortunate, that she had a home to move to," Carrie said, encouraging the woman. Carrie, recently divorced from her second husband, hadn't been as lucky when her marriage dissolved.

"Yes," Lucy said. "Where is this home?"

"In Venice. On Calle del Milion. It had been in the family for, let me see…I think five, maybe six generations."

While that was unheard of in the States, Lucy knew it was how things were done in many parts of Italy. Homes stayed in the family, handed down from one generation to the next.

"Do you know her husband's name? For that matter, what was Aurelia's surname?" Lucy asked, hoping she wasn't pushing too far.

Signora Di Votti didn't seem alarmed by the questions and readily answered, "Carotti. She was Aurelia Carotti. Her no-good husband is Enzo." The way she said the man's name Lucy expected her to spit on the paving stones after speaking it.

She noticed Oscar had wandered down the *calle*. He looked like he was wishing he had his camera—which he'd left in the backroom—to take shots of the brilliant red geraniums in the window sills and of the washing hanging outside the upper windows on the brightly painted homes across the narrow *calle*. A young boy rode a bicycle toward them, stopping at the house directly across from where they stood. He jumped off the bike and dropped it to the stones before entering his home.

"Does Enzo live in Venice, too?" Lucy asked.

"*Sì*. They shared a flat near Santi Giovanni e Paolo," she said with a loud sigh.

"Is that a neighborhood?" Carrie asked.

"Church," Signora Di Votti told her, sounding peeved that Carrie wouldn't know such an obvious fact.

Lucy decided not to push any further. She had enough information to begin a small investigation of her own.

Her timing was perfect, because at that moment two Carabinieri appeared in the doorway. There was no getting around it, they were imposing in their military camouflage uniforms with the burgundy caps, and Lucy clenched her teeth at the sight of them.

One said something in Italian, and Signora Di Votti stepped inside, waving at Lucy to follow.

Once inside, again in the backroom, the officer turned his attention to Lucy, and in clear, heavily accented English asked to see her passport.

Lucy removed her passport from the interior zippered pocket

in her purse and handed it to the Carabinieri officer without making eye contact. As she'd dressed that morning, she'd decided against keeping it in a money belt as she should have, knowing access to it under a dress would be impossible. She gave herself a mental pat on the back for being so foresighted.

He flipped to the I.D. page and studied it carefully, looking up at the living version a few times, obviously verifying what he was reading.

When he seemed to be satisfied he closed the passport but didn't return it to Lucy.

He asked Lucy to tell him everything from the time she left the lace shop to the time he had arrived on the scene at the canal.

When she had finished her careful recitation of the events, he asked, "How was it you were at the canal to see the body? So soon after you claimed to have left this shop?" The words were curt, and Lucy doubted it had anything to do with the difference in languages.

Lucy looked him square in the eye. The man looked to be in his thirties and was male-model handsome. "As I said," she began, fighting the instinct to show her irritation at the question, "my friends and I were just crossing the bridge at the canal when we heard screams. I wanted to see why people were screaming. I could see them by the canal."

"Do you always go where you hear screams?"

"No. Of course not," Lucy barked at the irritating officer and his question. "But I worked for a police department in the States for many years."

"You were a police officer?"

Lucy squirmed. "No. I worked as a civilian." Having to admit that distressed her, so she quickly added, "But I did go through the academy before deciding that working the streets didn't suit me."

He handed her passport to the other officer. "We'll record your information, and then you are free to go. Thank you," he said without inflection.

Lucy's eyes flickered from one to the other of her friends as she waited for the other man to write her name, address, and passport number in a small flip style notebook.

By the time he handed her the passport the other officer was deep into his questioning of Aurelia's employer. Lucy tried to catch her eye before they left but was unable to. Before anyone could decide to keep them any longer they hurried out of the shop.

"We will have to come back to Burano at some point," Lucy pointed out to the group as they waited for their lunch orders at an outdoor cafe on the *piazza*. She had her day planner open, searching for a free time during the coming several days.

"Just make sure you pick a day the museum is actually open this time," Carrie quipped as she lifted her glass of red wine to her lips.

Keeping her eyes on the calendar, Lucy replied evenly, "Of course. But do keep in mind this is Italy, not the U. S., and they might not quite keep to the rigid schedule we are accustomed to."

Oscar shifted his body and leaned in to focus on Lucy. "Lucy, are you really planning to go off looking for this murderer? Because if you are, I think I'd like to hang here for a while and get as much footage as I can."

Hester answered before Lucy could finish her swallow of wine. "I think that sounds like a good idea, Oscar." She allowed her eyes to rest on him briefly before she continued. "Yes, Lucy does want to check into a few things, and I'm going along with her. Carrie, what do you want to do?"

Carrie turned to Lucy. "You said you have my script done for Burano, right?"

"Yeah."

"Maybe I should stay behind with Oscar and do some of the scenes today. Then when we come back we can just fill in the museum parts and anything else we aren't ready to do today."

They spent the next several minutes on logistics, and only put it aside when their lunches were served.

Lucy and Hester both had polenta topped with the sweetest, most delicate tiny shrimp either of them had ever tasted. Oscar dove into his massive bowl of seafood fettuccine brimming with mussels and clams in their shells, shrimp, and slices of octopus. All most likely caught not far from where they were enjoying their meal. Carrie savored a fresh Caprese salad.

After lunch they agreed to meet up at the hotel at five o'clock, or as Carrie now liked to refer to it, Spritz o'clock, after her new favorite Venetian cocktail.

Just before parting from the full group, Carrie put a hand

on Oscar's shoulder. "So, what do you say to finding some gelato before we get to work?"

He readily agreed, and like two children they skipped off, visions of gelato most likely dancing in their heads.

Lucy and Hester headed to the docks to pick up the water taxi Hester had ordered during lunch. As she trudged to the dock, Lucy imagined the sweet, refreshing gelato her friends were about to enjoy. The day had become uncomfortably warm, and gelato sounded like the perfect salve.

On the boat, with salty *laguna* water spraying on them every time the water taxi encountered a wake from another boat, they discussed how best to proceed with the investigation.

Lucy said, "My guess would be that the local detective, from the main island of Venice, will just now be heading to Burano to begin his or her investigation of the crime scene. I doubt he'll have anyone doing anything yet in Venice proper. So let's try to find the husband first, then I really want to try to get into her house before the day is over."

Hester, who had a dribble of the shrimp's butter sauce on her dress, gave her friend a long look.

"Sounds a touch illegal."

"Not necessarily. Not if someone lets us in."

"And just how do you think you'll manage that?"

"We'll see," Lucy answered, mysteriously. In truth, it was just as much of a mystery to Lucy.

~ four ~

LUCY AND HESTER DISEMBARKED AT the magnificent Piazza San Marco, the most popular tourist magnet in Venice. And as such, the mass of humanity that crowded the waterfront and the entrance to the square made it difficult for the two women to make their way into, and then across, the square itself.

With the massive, impressive, pastiche Basilica of San Marco with its mishmash of Gothic and Byzantine architecture looming over them they managed to cut across to a narrow *calle* near the clocktower. As she admired the blue clock face decorated with gold Zodiac signs and stars, Lucy made a mental note to have Oscar photograph the mystical looking, ancient clock.

Lucy led the way through the maze of crowded, narrow walkways, becoming lost only once. Fifteen minutes after leaving San Marco they turned a corner and saw on the other side of a canal the Campo Santi Giovanni e Paolo.

With a dramatic wave of her hand, Lucy proudly announced, "And here we are!"

They crossed the bridge into the famous *campo* or small square. Unlike the dark, narrow, labyrinthine walkways that wend their way between the city's medieval and Renaissance buildings, the open *campo* was bathed in sunlight. Recalling the research she had done on Venice's *campi*, she knew the stone-paved squares that dotted the city made for gathering places for the neighbors who lived around them.

Lucy pointed out the dark brick church of Saints Giovanni and Paolo, and the much more impressive white marble facade of Scuola Grande di San Marco.

Pointing at the Scuola, Lucy said, "You, my brilliant friend, might want to go in there sometime while we're in Venice. Among other things, there's a museum on the history of medicine. Right up your alley." She laughed and poked her friend in the side. "Probably has body parts in jars and everything!" she said as she rubbed her hands together in a display of fake glee.

Acting affronted, Hester said, "Actually, that does sound interesting. Perhaps I shall find the time."

When Hester then turned her back on Lucy, Lucy noticed a price tag hanging out of the neckline of Hester's dress.

She chose to let it go without comment.

Lucy surveyed the square, its buildings, a tall white marble monument atop of which stood a statue of a Renaissance man on a horse, and shops and cafes, looking for the right place to make inquiries.

"See that cafe on the corner there? Let's go ask if anyone knows Enzo. I'm guessing that as a resident of the area, someone there might know him."

Hester followed Lucy over to the cafe, where several of the outdoor tables had diners sitting at them. Two waiters scurried around the tables, bringing menus, plates of food, and drinks to the hungry tourists.

Lucy knew they wouldn't have to wait long before a waiter came over to help them—Hester had a way of being noticed, especially by men. Hester, on the other hand, was oblivious to the attention she'd received daily since she'd hit the age of sixteen and grew into her Nordic beauty. And now, at the age of forty-five, she looked closer to thirty-five.

A handsome young man nearly skipped over to Hester as soon as his eyes lit on her. His broad smile and shining eyes were precisely what Lucy expected to see.

"*Buongiorno!* Would you like a table, *signora*?"

Hester graced him with a dazzling smile, her perfect white teeth only marred by the bit of herb that had adhered itself to an upper front tooth.

"Perhaps later. Your food looks *delizioso.* We are looking for a friend of a friend of ours."

Lucy grinned to herself, impressed by Hester's acumen for lying. Then she took over.

"Yes, we are hoping to find a man named Enzo Carotti. He lives near here."

The waiter's eyes flickered from Lucy to the more stunning Hester.

"*Mi dispiace.* I am sorry. But I am…new here. I will get Gino to talk to you," he said in halting English.

They watched as he sauntered over to the other waiter,

who listened to his tale before looking up at Hester and beaming.

The second waiter wasted no time hurrying to her side.

Lucy explained that they were looking for the man named Enzo Carotti. All the while she spoke the waiter's eyes were on Hester.

"Enzo, you say?" he asked, with a quick glance at Lucy.

"Yes. Enzo Carotti."

"Yes, I know this man."

"Where could we find him?"

He pointed around the corner of the building in which the cafe was located. "Down the *fondamenta*, there. It ends just a little way down and there you go across the canal." The man struggled with the English. "Carotti's *casa* is four doors down on the right. Green door. His place on floor the third."

"That is most helpful," Hester said with a smile, which made the man grin. "*Grazie*."

"So, what exactly is a *fondamenta*?" Lucy asked Hester, as they left the cafe. "I've seen it on the maps I've had to study for this trip, but where exactly are we supposed to be going?"

"It's just the word they use for the walkways that are right along a canal." She began to lead the way to the *fondamenta* in question.

Once they were on the side of the building, they found themselves walking along a narrow strip of alleyway. One false step would have landed them in the canal. The reflection of the water danced along the side of the building, lighting up what would otherwise have been a dark, forbidding alleyway.

The *fondamenta* dead-ended less than twenty-five feet from the corner of the building, forcing them to cross the bridge over the canal. The *calle* it led them to was exceptionally narrow—they had to walk single file as they counted doors. Graffiti had been spray painted here and there on the walls—walls with crumbling plaster that exposed the ancient brick beneath.

Lucy had noticed the crumbling plaster on buildings throughout the sections of Venice they had seen, and found it charming. Part of the Venetian beauty. Whereas, had it been at home in California, she would have thought it nothing more than derelict.

They came to the fourth door, but it was black. The next one was several feet further and painted a dark green.

Lucy tried the door, knowing it would be locked. She wasn't disappointed. A buzzer hung on the wall next to the door, and she pressed it.

The doorknob clicked, and Hester pushed it open.

They stepped into the gloom of the interior, the only light coming from a small transom above the door. Directly in front of them stood a tall, steep staircase. As there were no other choices, they started to climb the stone stairs.

At the first landing they found a door, but continued up the next flight, remembering that Enzo lived on the third floor.

As Lucy began to pant near the top of the second flight of steep stairs, Hester cheerfully said, "Remember, in

Europe, the second floor is called the first, and the third is the second, so we have to go to the fourth floor."

"Oh, jolly fun," Lucy spat. "I think my thigh muscles are feeling all those bridge stairs from yesterday." She knew she should never have allowed her gym membership to lapse. But Lucy was of the mind that exercise was the most boring activity known to humankind.

"Ah, just think how strong you're getting."

Lucy admonished herself for not having thrown Hester into the Grand Canal when she'd had the chance.

Finally at the top of the building, standing before the door to Enzo's flat, Lucy held up an index finger begging for a moment to catch her breath.

Before they had a chance to knock on the door, it swung open.

Staring at them, mouth hanging open, stood a man about Lucy's height, whose age was difficult to determine. The T-shirt he wore showed off a fit body, but the lines on his face indicated a life lived hard.

He barked something in Italian which Lucy didn't understand, but she certainly could translate the anger emanating from him and took a small step back. A larger step would have plunged her down the stairs.

Hester said something back to him in Italian, as he pushed his way past them.

As he started down the stairs he growled something back at Hester, and Lucy heard the name Aurelia a couple of times.

The two women stood on the small landing and watched him stomp down the stairs.

"That would be Enzo Carotti," Hester said, rather unnecessarily. "He just had a visit from the police and is now going to identify the body of his wife."

Lucy pursed her lips, thinking. "Not exactly broken up with grief, is he?"

"No."

"Pretty angry about it."

"I'd say so. He made it sound like the identification was an imposition."

"Really? Hmmm…what did you say to explain our visit?"

"Not much, he didn't exactly allow me to talk. All I managed to say was that we were there to talk to him about Aurelia."

"And we're a couple of complete strangers," Lucy said as she thought it through. "And we're asking about his wife, whom he just found out is dead, and he's not the least bit curious why we want to talk to him?"

"You think that's odd?"

"I think that's odd. Yes. Though I suppose it could be some cultural difference."

They fell silent for a minute.

Then, Lucy added, "Or…he already knew his wife was dead because he killed her. So any dealings with the police are a potential problem for him, and that's all he could think about. Our presence was unimportant to him."

"Perhaps we should ask around, to the neighbors and such, and find out more about Enzo."

"Agreed. But first, I want to get to that house of Aurelia's. I doubt we'll run into the local police there if they haven't even had the body officially ID'd yet."

They started down the stairs, and Lucy began to hum softly.

Santa Lucia.

"A little operatic deja vu?" Hester asked with a wry smile.

"Oh, was I humming?" Lucy feigned innocence.

"You know you were."

"Huh. How about that."

Lucy gave her friend a wink.

When they'd arrived back in the *calle*, Lucy turned to Hester. "I sure hope your phenomenal memory stored away the name of the *calle* where Aurelia lived."

"And what will you give me in return?"

"Oh, let's see…" Lucy rubbed her chin. "How about a little orchestrated alone time with Oscar?"

Hester's Nordic complexion reddened.

Lucy was the only person to know of Hester's long-hidden feelings for Oscar.

Feelings that went back to the first day he walked into Chess Club during their freshman year in high school. And feelings that had been shelved for the many years the four lived in different regions of the world. Until they'd gathered five months earlier to hear Hester present her idea for the company they now were trying to launch.

"Lucy! Hush."

"Hester, my dear, dear friend, we are forty-five years old. I have one marriage behind me, Carrie has two. And you still won't tell the poor man that you're desperately in love with him?"

Hester put her perfect, straight nose in the air. "I'll know when the time is right."

"And you don't think that time together in one of the most romantic cities in the world is the *right* time?"

She casually shrugged. "I don't know. Perhaps. Or perhaps Paris will be the best place for such an admission."

"Tick tock…So, where are we going?"

"Signora Di Votti said it was on Calle del Milion."

Lucy took her iPad out of her satchel and looked up Calle del Milion.

Peering at the tablet, she said, "North of the Rialto Bridge, this side of the Grand Canal. And we have a landmark we can use to find our way."

The walls of Venice are covered with signs directing lost tourists to the most visited destinations in the city. Lucy had heard that they could come in handy when attempting to navigate the network of *calli* in Venice.

"And what would that be?"

Lucy grinned mischievously. "One we have on our itinerary, actually. Marco Polo's home. Aurelia's house is just down the street."

Lucy chuckled to herself.

If someone had told her a year ago that one day she would be zipping over to Marco Polo's house, she would have called them daft.

~ five ~

A HALF AN HOUR AFTER leaving Enzo's flat near Campo Santi Giovanni di Paolo, Lucy and Hester were still looking for Marco Polo's home. Despite the best satellite maps online they made numerous wrong turns and finally paused in a *campo* near the Rialto Bridge to regroup. Several local boys were kicking a soccer ball around the small square, their squeals and shouts piercing the air.

"Now," Lucy said with all the authority she could muster. "Everything I've read about Venice has said that getting lost is part of the charm of Venice and to be expected. All these narrow alleyways and canals and dead ends are what makes the adventure." She hoped that by saying the words, they would become the truth. At the moment she wasn't sure how she felt about this particular adventure. Lucy had always been one to map out everywhere she went—surprises when attempting to get from point A to point B did not, in general, bring her great joy.

With her usual boundless cheer, Hester said, "I agree! I love the feel of Venice, the smell, the sounds, the old world charm. I'm not worried about how long this takes us."

"Well, actually, I kind of am. Since we have to find Aurelia's home, find someone to let us in, and then get back out all before the police show up."

"Oh. You do make an excellent point. Here, may I look at that for a minute?"

Lucy happily handed over the iPad.

Hester mumbled to herself as she peered at the satellite map. "Okay, Ponte di Rialto is right here, then we need to cut across this *campo*, follow the *calle* to that bridge there, and keep going straight until we start seeing signs for the Marco Polo house. We'll be taking a right somewhere along there." She looked up from the tablet with a grin. "Got it, follow me."

Five minutes later they were following a sign to the famous house when Lucy looked up on the side of a building to see a sign that announced they had found their destination, Calle del Milion.

She grabbed Hester, who was already marching down the next narrow alleyway.

"Whoa, girl. I think we're here."

Hester's gaze followed Lucy's pointing finger.

"Voila!" Lucy exclaimed. "And how convenient that there's a bar right here where we can ask about Aurelia's home. I've read that everyone knows everyone within the neighborhoods here. Comes from having no cars and having to walk everywhere. It worked with Enzo's place and I think it should here, too."

They stepped under the bar's red awning and into the

quiet business. Only one person, an elderly man, stood at the bar sipping an espresso. The aroma of espresso hit Lucy, making her salivate.

Hearing the woman working the bar speaking rapid Italian or Venetian to the man with the espresso, Lucy motioned Hester to do the talking.

In Italian—even Hester didn't speak Venetian—she inquired about the location of Aurelia Carotti's home.

With much gesturing and rapid-fire words, the woman told Hester how to find it.

"*Grazie mille*," Hester said when the woman finally stopped speaking.

"Follow me," she said with a mischievous grin.

Outside the bar Hester stopped, and facing the bar, pointed up.

"There."

Above the bar stood the most charming, quintessentially Venetian building with freshly painted classic green Venetian shutters, window boxes overflowing with flowers, and a small terrace on top of the bar with an arbor on which grapes grew. The top floor consisted of a larger terrace with a wrought iron fence running around it. Several planter boxes sat on top of the fence. Most of the brick on the building was exposed, with only a few places still sporting the original plaster.

"The third floor, or second, is hers."

Lucy pointed at the building. "You mean the one right below the terrace?"

"Yes."

"It looks like some of those windows are open. I don't think Aurelia would have left them open all day while she was at work. I wonder if there's someone in there?"

"Signora Di Votti didn't mention a roommate."

Lucy sucked on her lips then pursed them, repeating the nervous tic several times.

She took a deep breath when she stopped the tic. "Let's go up and see if anyone's home. If there is, then we have our entry. Easy peasy."

The outside, ground floor door was a double door, painted a bright red. Assuming it was locked Lucy went straight to the buzzer and pressed it. Several seconds later the door unlocked and they went in.

Unlike Enzo's building, this one had a proper foyer that was brightly illuminated by a window that looked out on a small atrium. A web of cracks throughout the marble floor indicated its age as well as the continual motion of Venice.

Hester took in the room, saying, "I'm sure this building was once a rather nice *palazzo*. Not one of the enormous, grand ones, but certainly home to someone with some degree of wealth."

Like the floor, the stairs were also marble, and the two women started up the lovely, ancient staircase.

On what the two Americans would call the third floor they stood in a large open landing. A small spiral staircase, made of wrought iron, led further up to the terrace. In front of them was the door to Aurelia's flat.

Lucy rapped on the door with enough force that anyone

inside would have to hear her. There was no doorbell anywhere near the door.

A minute later she knocked again.

After giving it another minute, Lucy exchanged a glance with Hester and reached out to the large, crystal doorknob. Trying it, Lucy found that it turned.

Drawing on the small amount of Italian she'd learned before they left for this adventure, she called out, "*Permesso?*" hoping that was indeed the word that translated into asking permission to enter, something required in Italy whenever going into someone's home. Though it was typically used when someone actually opened the door for the visitor, not when breaking and entering.

She knew that Hester would know, but was hoping that on this one occasion she could show off her one bit of knowledge. When Hester didn't correct her, Lucy smiled to herself.

They stepped in, and Lucy repeated her request for permission to enter, but the word only bounced off the walls of the flat, unanswered.

Lucy and Hester found themselves in a gracious room that could have been taken from a previous century if it were not for the large screen TV on one of the pale yellow painted walls. The floor beneath their feet was the traditional Venetian speckled flooring, made of marble fragments in hues of red, green, and cream. A deep red rug covered the floor between a sofa and two chairs. A Venetian glass chandelier hung in the center of the space. At the far end of the room a small, rough-hewn dining table stood with a vase of flowers sitting in the center of it.

"We probably don't have much time so let's move quickly. Zip through this room and the kitchen and then find Aurelia's bedroom," Lucy directed.

The small galley kitchen had recently been remodeled with modern cupboards and appliances. The only bathroom was large enough that it had probably started life as a bedroom. On a shelf in the bathroom were all the usual shampoos, lotions and the like. Lucy noticed two different brands of shampoo, as well as two brands of lotion.

"There's a roommate. We need to find a way to figure out which bedroom is Aurelia's."

They found three bedrooms, two obviously lived in, and one kept ready for a visitor.

Lucy chose the largest of the three bedrooms to search first. First, she needed to find something to ascertain that it was indeed Aurelia's room. Second, she would look for anything that could be a clue in her murder.

On a small dresser she found what she needed to determine that this was indeed Aurelia's room. What looked like a utility bill lay on it, and though Lucy couldn't read anything it said, she could read the name Aurelia Carotti at the top.

Also on the dresser top sat an antique brush and mirror, a picture of a young boy, an old-fashioned address book, a perfume bottle, and a jewelry box. Lucy opened the jewelry box but found nothing unexpected among the earrings, necklaces, and bracelets.

Then she flipped open the address book, which appeared to have been in use recently. The ink on some of the entries looked to be fresh, unfaded. She took out her phone and used its camera to quickly snap pictures of each page. Her eye landed on the photograph of the young boy again, and she took a picture of it and the other items on the dresser top, as well.

Lucy pointed to a wall of cupboards of varying sizes. "Let's start going through these."

Hester began with the smaller cupboards placed high on the wall, out of Lucy's reach, while Lucy went through one of the larger ones made for hanging clothing.

Beyond the expected clothes, she found a locked metal box at the back of the cupboard. She lifted it and gave it a little shake. Nothing rattled. Most likely important papers.

The contents of the next cupboard Lucy opened were less expected. Colorful, extravagantly festooned ball gowns hung in this one. She carefully removed one and held it up for Hester to see.

"What do you make of this? There's four of these in here."

"*Carnevale*, Carnival," she said as she ran her fingers over the feathers decorating the blue silk gown. "It's like New Orleans' Mardi Gras. Are there fancy masks in there?" Hester asked, excited by the find.

Lucy found boxes about the size of hatboxes on one side of the cupboard and removed one.

She opened it for Hester who held her hands clasped in front of her chest in anticipation.

Inside lay an elaborately decorated full-face mask that even included brightly painted lips. The only openings were for eyes and nostrils. Strings of beads hung from the sides, fake jewels and brocade were applied around the forehead and eyes, and around the mouth.

"Wow," they both said, making them giggle.

Lucy added, "Can you imagine wearing one of these? It would make for quite a night of intrigue." Her voice rose dramatically. An image of Nicolo, the opera singer, flashed through her mind.

The removal of the mask box had allowed Lucy to see a small section of the back of the cupboard.

"Something is back here," she told Hester. "Help me move these gowns and boxes."

They moved quickly to empty the cupboard.

Up against the back of the cupboard stood a large wooden crate. Lucy estimated it to be about three feet by four feet and about eight inches deep.

She took out her phone and turned on its flashlight. Using it, she got closer to the crate and examined it.

"Dusty," she reported to Hester. "But it's recently been moved because there're some spots where the dust has been disturbed." She looked over every visible inch. "I really, really want to see what's in here. It's hidden away. It's been unmoved until recently, and from the looks of the nails in the crate, it hasn't been opened in ages."

"What does all that mean?" Hester asked, though Lucy suspected she knew exactly what that meant.

Lucy slowly spoke as she thought through each bit. "It means that it's important to Aurelia, and that it's something she, and her family who lived here before her, didn't want anyone to find."

She stared at the box before finishing her thoughts.

"Then it was recently moved, and now Aurelia's been murdered."

~ six ~

"I DON'T KNOW HOW MUCH time we have, but I'm going to guess very little," Lucy stated the obvious.

"Do you think we should risk opening it?" Hester whispered.

"We'll never get another chance to, I'm sure. How do you feel about gambling with spending some time in an Italian prison?"

"I'd prefer not to have that experience, but I say we give it a try."

"Good, I vote for that too. I'm going to look for something to lift a couple of nails out with, and I think it would be best if you stand guard at the front door and listen for anyone coming up the stairs. But first, help me get this out of the closet."

Just before Hester put a hand on one of the corners, Lucy cried, "Wait!" She ran to the dresser and returned to the cupboard with four socks.

Handing Hester two, she said, "Put these on your hands. We can't leave any fingerprints."

Moving the crate slowly, they managed to get it out of the cupboard. Lucy closed the cupboard doors and propped the wooden box up against them.

Hester started for the front door while Lucy went in the kitchen and hoped Aurelia kept some tools in there.

It only took Lucy, who still wore the socks on her hands, a minute to find a hammer in a drawer in the modern kitchen.

Back in the bedroom, she used the claw end of the hammer to slowly pry out the three nails along the top of the crate.

Once they were out, she was able to gently lift the top panel up and off of the crate's frame.

She peered inside.

An old, dark-colored, woolen blanket appeared to be wrapped around something.

Knowing the crate hadn't been unusually heavy, Lucy tried to lift the item. It was not much heavier than the woolen blanket, and she was able to remove whatever it was with little trouble.

Keeping the item in the same position as it had been packed, Lucy gently lifted the blanket.

Throwing the blanket aside she gaped at a painting.

An ancient painting.

~ seven ~

"**H**ESTER?"

Lucy's voice cracked on the word. "Come here."

Lucy propped the painting against the crate while she waited for Hester. The woman whose many master's degrees from Oxford included one in art history.

Just before she got to the bedroom, Hester said, "What is it?"

Hester stepped into the room and froze.

Lucy stared at her friend and waited for her to show signs of life.

It took some time, but eventually Hester began taking slow, tentative steps toward the painting.

When she was finally in front of it, she flopped down, sat crossed legged, and leaned in close to it.

Lucy watched as tears formed in Hester's eyes.

"Oh. My. Lord," Hester said in a tone one usually

reserved for the interior of a magnificent church.

"I think I know what this is, Lucy."

Hester glanced up at Lucy, who still stood next to the painting, and nodded.

"And?" Lucy prompted.

Hester didn't answer immediately as she moved closer to the painting and peered at it—her eyes just inches from the canvas.

After minutes of close appraisal, Hester sat up, closed her eyes, and placed her hands over her mouth.

Lucy thought she might have been praying.

When Hester opened her eyes, she explained.

"I think…I think this is a famous, lost Canaletto. If I'm correct about what it is, this painting was stolen by the Nazis during World War Two and has been one of the hundreds, or thousands, of paintings never found. Some lists put this in the top ten missing works of art in the world."

Hearing that, Lucy joined Hester on the floor. It wasn't so much a case of wanting to get closer to the painting, as much as her legs having suddenly gone weak.

Hester took out her phone. "Let's get some good pictures of it, so that I can do some research. If I'm right, this is the biggest art discovery in decades." She began snapping pictures of the painting.

While Hester could only see a miraculous art discovery, Lucy could see a motive for murder.

"Okay, I appreciate that," Lucy told Hester. "But let's remember why and how and where we found it. This is part of a *murder investigation*."

Hester nodded grimly. "But it must be found. The police

must be made to discover it."

"I'm sure they will," Lucy assured her. "Right now, I'm beyond curious as to how this painting happens to be in this flat. Tell me a little about the painting. Who's Canaletto?"

"One of the great Venetian painters. I love his work. In fact, I think it was my love of Canaletto that made me decide to begin our adventure here in Venice. He was born in the late 1600's and painted for the first sixty or so years of the 1700's. Venice was his prime subject matter, but he also painted in Rome and if I'm not mistaken in Florence too. His paintings of the Venice canals are his most famous."

"I can see I'm going to want to learn more about this painter, but if you're finished taking pictures, I think it would be in our best interests to pack it back up and get the hell out of here before we're caught."

"Agreed." Hester gazed lovingly at the painting for a moment longer before standing and helping to replace the masterpiece just as they had found it, albeit without quite the same amount of dust covering the top of the crate.

They were returning the last of the Carnival ball gowns to the closet when they heard voices.

They ran out to the living room, and Hester peeked out the door.

"It sounds like they're still in the foyer," she reported.

"Good, let's go."

They exited the flat and pulled the door shut. When Hester began to walk to the staircase Lucy grabbed her by the arm.

"No," Lucy whispered. "Follow me."

Lucy began climbing the wrought iron spiral staircase that led to the rooftop terrace.

She sighed with relief when she found the door to the terrace unlocked. They stepped onto the roof.

All the way around the perimeter of the terrace, with its commanding view of the neighborhood and two different canals, were flower boxes planted with a variety of flowers that came in a spectacular array of colors. The brilliant blue sky made the perfect canopy to the view.

If they hadn't been hiding from the police, Lucy thought, they might have been able to more adequately appreciate the opportunity to enjoy such a view. But as it was, they found themselves standing stock still in the center of the terrace, in order to be invisible to anyone standing in the *calle* below, and so that they wouldn't make walking noises that could be heard in Aurelia's flat.

Ten minutes went by with them standing like Venetian statues on the terrace before Lucy became restless.

"I'm just going to tiptoe over to the railing there on the front side of the building. I want to see what's going on—if the police are out front too."

"Keep low," Hester admonished her. "They'll be able to see you if you're standing."

Lucy took slow, baby steps until she approached the point where she thought she would be seen, then crouched down low. Finally, she went down on her hands and knees and crawled the remainder of the way to the iron fencing, keeping her head behind a flower box.

The front of the building was quiet with only a couple of

tourists meandering down the *calle*. A young Italian man stood across the street, leaning against the wall of the building and smoking a cigarette. He seemed to be watching Aurelia's building.

With nothing to see, she crawled back to Hester. Hester put out a hand to help Lucy stand.

"I think now would be a good time to go down the stairs nonchalantly and on past the flat," Lucy said. "If the police see us it will simply look like a couple of women who were enjoying the terrace."

Hester, one of the few women on the face of the Earth to still wear a watch, glanced down at it. "And it's a quarter till five, and we need to get back to the hotel to meet with Carrie and Oscar."

"Indeed. We can't miss Spritz o'clock."

Hester, a lifelong teetotaler, had been convinced after their long arrival day to try the local drink as a cultural experience. Lucy had watched as her friend's face lit up with the first sip of the sweet, sparkling aperitif made of Prosecco and the bitter orange liqueur, Aperol. Sitting in the sun in the Piazza San Marco, the drink looked like sunshine itself. The classic cocktail for the iconic locale.

With Lucy leading the way, the women quietly made their way down the staircase and past the apartment where the door was ajar. They scooted past the door and wasted no time going down the two flights of stairs.

Back in the *calle,* they allowed themselves a bit of nervous laughter before Lucy was hit with reality.

"Now how do we get back to our hotel?"

Hester grinned at her lopsidedly. "Give me the iPad. Leave this one to me."

Lucy reached into her bag and turned over the iPad, then stuck her hand back in and brought out her security blanket, thought-booster, and addiction.

A cinnamon flavored Jolly Rancher lollipop.

She ripped off the wrapper and placed the candy in her mouth.

And immediately, she felt up to the task of finding the way home.

~ eight ~

WITH ONLY TWO WRONG TURNS along the way, Lucy and Hester found their way back to the hotel in less than twenty minutes. It was a small, family-run Venetian hotel not far from the opera house. The opera house where Nicolo Gavelli would be singing that very night. Lucy wished they didn't have to wait a few more days for that treat.

After freshening up, the two women went down to the minuscule lobby to wait for Carrie and Oscar. Only two chairs sat in the small area by the front desk, and they both fell into the chairs with loud sighs of relief.

The reprieve was interrupted far too soon for Lucy's liking. Oscar and Carrie bounced into the room looking ready to take on the Venetian evening.

"We got some good stuff," Carrie crowed.

Oscar silently nodded his agreement.

Carrie focused on Lucy and asked, "Did you two find anything interesting?" Lucy noted, with a touch of irritation, that Carrie had made it sound like she was referring to travel discoveries rather than murder investigation discoveries.

Before Lucy could answer, Hester effused, "Oh my gosh, you would never believe it! Yes, we did indeed find something interesting."

"Listen, if it's okay with all of you, I thought we might go somewhere quiet and have a drink while we go over tomorrow's plans," Lucy suggested. "And while we're relaxing Hester and I can tell you about our exciting afternoon."

"Sounds good to me," Oscar happily agreed.

"Oscar, would you mind getting your camera?" Lucy asked. "If *The Money* is okay with some extra expense," she looked to Hester imploringly, "I thought we could have cocktails in Caffè Florian."

"*Oh yes!*" Carrie quickly agreed. "But don't you think some filming would be a good idea?"

"I thought I'd ask what their rules are when we get there. I think that for now it would be nice if Oscar can get some photos of the sumptuous interior. That would be a good start. And besides, if we're filming it should be earlier in the day when people are drinking espressos."

"Okay, sounds good to me."

"Good plan, Lucy," Hester said. "So to Piazza San Marco we go." Hester was again in cheerleader mode. The sweetness of her tone made Lucy's teeth hurt.

As soon as Oscar had run up to his room to retrieve his camera they took off to the square. The night before, the foursome had enjoyed Venetian cocktails in the open air of the square, but Caffè Florian was an altogether different experience.

After the short walk to the square, they walked along the arcade that runs around three sides of the *piazza*. The fourth side, without any arcade, is where the massive San Marco Basilica and its neighbor, The Doge's Palace, are located.

At this hour most of the Florian customers were seated outside where they could enjoy the scene on the square as well as the live music right outside the caffè. Lucy figured the inside of the iconic coffee house would be fairly quiet. Plus it was the magnificent Caffè Florian.

Opened in the early 1700's, the interior of the caffè is done in Neo-Baroque style, making for a lavish, over-the-top decor. Made up of several rooms, there is gilding everywhere, paintings throughout, and massive mirrors in gilt frames, with round or oblong marble tables and red velvet banquettes and chairs in each room.

After they were seated in a room that could have been lifted right out of a palace, along the lines of Versailles, they ordered Spritz Aperols all around.

It took little time in the room filled with mirrors for Lucy to conclude that a place with that many mirrors was an affront to womankind. Her reflection continually beamed itself at her, and she was less than pleased with what she saw. With her eye on a mirror, she tugged at a wayward bit of hair, trying to force it to behave and return to its rightful place. It was an exercise in futility, and she deflated with a loud sigh. Any makeup she might have applied that morning seemed to have disappeared. The face she gaped at looked old and haggard.

Forcing her eyes away from her many reflected images,

and reminding herself she had a job to do, Lucy focused her attention on her friends. "So, when I was doing research, I read that back in Casanova's day, this was the only public meeting place where women were welcome, which made it the perfect place for Casanova to pick up women."

Carrie's mouth fell open. "Casanova used to hang out here?"

"Yep," Lucy said, as she opened her day planner and took out a pen.

When she saw her friends all gaping at their surroundings, Lucy put her pen down and joined them for a moment.

But someone needed to focus the group, so eventually, Lucy said, "Okay, for tomorrow we have the guided tour of the basilica in the morning," she began reciting the day's schedule. Not until they were all clear on expectations for the next day, from the tour of the church to the tour of La Fenice Opera house, did she feel she could divulge hers and Hester's afternoon adventures.

Just as Lucy finished up with the schedule, their drinks arrived, along with a small bowl of peanuts, another filled with tortilla chips, and a third containing green olives.

They lifted their drinks, tapping the glasses together while wishing each other "Cincin," the Italian version of 'cheers.'

"So...Hester wasn't lying. We had quite the interesting afternoon."

"That would be an understatement," Hester chimed in.

They told Carrie and Oscar about finding Aurelia's husband, then their trek across the island in search of her family home while using Marco Polo's house as a landmark.

This earned a chuckle from Oscar. "Marco, Freakin' Polo's house. That's brilliant. Love it. We'll want pictures, right?"

"Yes. But wait," Hester said, raising an index finger— signaling him to be quiet.

Lucy turned the tale of finding the probable Canaletto and its history over to Hester to share.

By the time they had finished their story, both Carrie and Oscar appeared stunned.

"You mean, not only could it be a clue to a motive in this murder, but it could be a really, really big time art discovery and story?" Carrie stammered.

"It could be," Hester said. "I'm assuming the police found it today, but we'll see."

"You know," Lucy said, "I'd really like to know if they did find it. Any ideas how we can find out? I mean without implicating ourselves in breaking and entering."

The other three stared at one another in turn.

Lucy watched as Hester tapped her right index finger on the marble tabletop, a tic she recognized. Whenever Hester was deep in thought, she tapped. And always with the same finger. Had she analyzed it closer she would have discovered that Hester always tapped at the exact same rate and cadence. A metronome couldn't have kept better time.

A minute later a smile played at Hester's mouth. "I

believe I may have a way to find out what the police have discovered."

Hester watched as three pairs of eyes stared at her expectantly.

"I have a guide friend here in town. Lucy knows who I mean because we'll be using her as a guide for some of our research here. In fact, she'll be taking us through the Basilica tomorrow morning."

"Yeah, so?" Carrie spat. "What good is a guide going to be at getting police information?" She tossed a peanut into her mouth.

"This particular guide has a sister-in-law who's with the local police. She may be of help to us."

"Please remind me, Hester," Lucy began. "How well do you know this guide? I'm just wondering if perhaps such a request might be a bit beyond her comfort zone."

"Anna Dorini and I met at Oxford. She was studying there as well, and we had a couple of classes together. We became pretty good friends. I think she might be willing to help us."

"Worth a try, I suppose," Lucy conceded.

Carrie gave a tentative nod, and Oscar shrugged.

"I know it's still early for dinner—here in Italy, anyway." Hester said. "But it's going on seven, and I know I'm starving. There's supposed to be a fantastic restaurant just on the other side of the opera house. What do you say?"

Oscar stood. "I, for one, am famished. Let me find our waiter and get the check."

Ten minutes later the foursome, now relaxed after the aperitifs, was winding its way through the intricate web of *calli*, in search of the restaurant.

Lucy was happy to be led by the others, as her mind was occupied elsewhere, hoping that they could indeed find a helpful person inside the local police department. She needed to know more about the painting. She was certain it was a key to finding Aurelia's murderer.

A well-fed, satiated Lucy was getting comfortable in her hotel room, listening to the deafening silence outside her open windows and appreciating the peace that prevails when there are no cars within a city's limits, when there was a soft knock on the door. She glanced at her phone—ten-fifteen.

She padded across the floor to the door.

"Yes?" she said through the closed door.

"It's Oscar. Let me in."

Lucy had to appreciate Oscar's straightforward manner. There was no wasting words with Oscar.

She opened the door.

"What's up?"

As he stepped into the room, he said, "I was just going through what I shot today, on video, and I think I might have caught the murderer on—geez your room is bigger than mine. Lots bigger."

He did a turn in the middle of the room, taking it all in, from the elegant Venetian wall covering, to the modest Murano glass chandelier, to the queen-sized bed, to the small marble top table and two chairs by the large window. "My room is more like a large closet with a super narrow twin bed." Oscar didn't try to hide his disappointment.

"Oscar…please focus. What's this about the murderer? In your video?"

"Yeah. Yeah." He gave himself a little shake. "I was just running through the stuff I shot while you were looking for a lacemaker. That canal where the body was found is off in the distance in one shot, but you can kind of see someone leaning over the canal like they're looking in it, *or like they just put a body in it*, and then they walk away."

"Really?" Lucy squealed. "Can you show it to me?"

"Sure. Come on over to my wee, tiny room, and if I can fit both of us in it, I'll show you the clip."

Lucy grabbed her room key and followed Oscar out the door.

As they walked down one flight of stairs, Lucy said, "You know, Oscar, that Hester wants us to have unique travel experiences in a variety of accommodations, everywhere we travel. That's the only way we can properly report on the hotels. I'm sure we will all have our turns staying in large rooms and small rooms. Plus, don't forget, we aren't using American style hotels. We want the real Italian hotel experience while we're here in Venice."

Oscar's only answer was a grumble.

They arrived at room 6, and Oscar opened the door.

Lucy immediately saw that he had been right—the room was rather small, but it was clean and comfortable and had a lovely view out onto the quiet *calle* below.

He stepped over to the desk where he'd set up his monitor. Lucy noted that he'd had to place the small TV on the floor in order to make room for his equipment.

Oscar pulled out the chair and told Lucy to have a seat.

"Now remember, this is from a distance, and if I work on it later I might be able to zoom in and do something about the graininess, but watch right there." He tapped the frozen image on the screen indicating the edge of the canal. Then he started the video, in slow motion.

Lucy watched intently. A figure stood next to the canal, right where Aurelia's body had been found. As she peered at the monitor, she saw the person lean forward, over the canal. Then it slowly stood, put its hands in the pockets of a hoodie, turned to the left and walked out of the camera view.

Oscar replayed the footage.

The figure wore dark pants, maybe jeans, but it was hard to tell from the poor quality of the image. The hoodie was dark, too, and the hood was up, obscuring the face and hair. From what she could see Lucy thought the person looked to be of medium height and build. It was impossible to tell if the person was male or female. As the image stood now, un-enhanced by Oscar, it was impossible to see anything that would lead anyone to the killer.

If, indeed, this was the killer.

Lucy sat up.

"Huh," she said. "I suppose that might be the murderer, or it might simply be someone looking in the canal. And we can't really see much of him or her."

"But isn't that right where you saw the body?"

"Yeah." Lucy fell silent for a moment. "If the body was there, then this person had to have seen it. Who sees a body floating in a canal and then just moseys off, all casual with their hands in their pockets as if it was nothing out of the ordinary?"

Oscar nodded once. "Exactly. That person had to have seen the body. But they didn't react to it—at all. I'd say no reaction means they're the one to put the body there."

"I tend to agree. Can you do much with that footage with the equipment you have here?" Lucy asked the question fearing the answer.

"A little. But if I want to do much more with it, I'll need to get into a studio somewhere that has the kind of equipment I'd need to be able to do a really good job on it."

"Well, for now, can you see how much you can enhance the image? I know you're tired, but would it be possible for you to get started on it tonight?"

"Sure, no problem. What I can do here won't take that long. I should be able to show it to you tomorrow morning."

"Thank you, Oscar. I appreciate that."

He let Lucy know it was time for her to leave by making wide, swinging arm motions toward the door.

"Yep, good-night Oscar. I'm outta here."

As Lucy shut the door, she saw Oscar already peering at the screen and pushing a few keys on his keyboard.

If, and she knew it was a big *if*, Oscar could clear up that image, this would be a welcome, and unexpected, break in the case.

She skipped up the flight of stairs as if she were a regular at the gym. There was no sign of the recalcitrant traveler who had moaned as she had to cross canal bridges the day before.

∽ nine ∽

LUCY SURREPTITIOUSLY REMOVED HER SHOE under the table where they sat in the late morning sun in Piazza San Marco. She stretched her toes and flexed the foot that had spent too many hours standing in and shuffling through the impressive Basilica San Marco. As soon as she finished with that sore foot, she turned her attention to the other. The shoes didn't go with the navy capris and crisp white blouse she wore, but she'd known that fashion was going to have to give way to function on these trips.

Following Anna Dorini's excellent tour through the church, the group, including Anna, had voted for an espresso in the square. Lucy had already made up her mind that she didn't care what anyone else wanted to do, she was going to sit for a half an hour and get off her complaining feet. She could put the time to good use going through the copious notes she'd made during the tour and sketching out the outline for the San Marco section of the Venice article. The article that would go into their first, slick travel magazine.

She had never in her life seen anything like the basilica. The interior was not at all what she'd expected. Had she been in Istanbul, perhaps she wouldn't have been surprised by the architecture and decor. But in Venice, it came as a shock.

Virtually every inch of the walls and dome was covered in gold mosaics. They had walked in at a time when the lights were not yet on, and Lucy had been disappointed by the apparent drabness of what she saw. But at the time that they turned on the lights for the daily illumination, she felt as if she'd stepped into heaven itself. The place glowed. Within the glittering gold, Biblical stories were illustrated in colored tiles. The Byzantine church also led to a feeling of stepping back in time. Quite a ways back.

Cameras and all photography are not allowed in the church, but professional photographers are able to apply for a permit, so prior to leaving for the trip Lucy had arranged for Oscar to enter before the church officially opened for the day and take photos for a specified amount of time.

Anna had been a delightful tour guide and as the morning progressed Lucy began to feel more comfortable with the idea of asking for help with the local police. But as she sat in the sun sipping her Americano, she was beginning to have some misgivings.

Hester must have read her mind, because when there was a momentary lull in the conversation, she said, "Anna, we are wondering if you could do us a favor. It is quite unusual, and you are welcome to say no."

Anna, a woman in her late forties, was fashionably

dressed in gray tailored slacks, a cream jacket over a matching shell that was topped off by a brightly colored scarf. She narrowed one eye which focused on Hester like a laser.

"It's really for me," Lucy said.

The narrowed eye turned to Lucy. "You see, we happened upon a murder victim yesterday—"

Anna let out a gasp and a string of Italian words that Lucy assumed were words of shock and commiseration.

"Yes, it was most unfortunate. Quite upsetting," Lucy said, stretching the truth for her purposes. "I was even interviewed by the Carabinieri." She hoped that the mention of the formidable military police would sway Anna. "You see, after seeing the poor woman's body in the canal I felt a connection—like I needed to do something. I have a background working with the police where we all live in California, and I might be interested in following this case. If that is at all possible."

She paused to gauge Anna's reaction to what she'd shared so far. Her brows formed a V between her eyes, but she didn't appear to be alarmed, so Lucy decided to continue.

"I understand you have a sister-in-law who works with the local police. I'm wondering if there's any way you could find out the status of the investigation and let me know."

The furrow between Anna's eyes deepened as she stared at Lucy, who wasn't disconcerted by the guide's expression. She'd seen much worse in her years with the police department.

Seconds ticked away while neither woman moved. While

the showdown continued, Carrie turned her attention to her phone. Hester flipped through the pages of her notebook. And Oscar began scrolling through images on his camera. Lucy took a casual sip of her coffee as she waited out Anna. Several seconds later she risked a glance at Anna and observed that the furrow had lessened.

"Well…" Anna broke the silence a few beats later. "I suppose I could ask Maria, but I cannot promise that she will be willing to do this that you ask."

"I understand, of course," Lucy said. "The cop in me just can't leave this horrible crime without knowing that justice will be served."

Anna made a small laughing sound. "You sound just like Maria. She can never rest until she's done all she can for the victims of crime."

Lucy nodded and smiled at Anna. "That's it exactly."

"I'll see what I can do." Lucy noted the change of attitude. Connecting. She'd learned long ago that nothing can be accomplished without first building feelings of connection with people. She and Anna had connected. She knew she was a step closer to getting the information she needed.

Anna returned her attention to the entire group. "I hear you are touring Teatro La Fenice this afternoon. You are in for a treat—the opera house is gorgeous." She placed a hand on her heart. "You know, of course, that it has burned down more than once. What you will see is quite new, rebuilt after a devastating fire in 1996, but it gives a grand, old-world feel. They rebuilt it to look just as it did prior to the fire. You will love it."

Hester told her about meeting Nicolo Gavelli, the opera singer, and how he was treating them to a performance while they were in Venice.

"Ahh…then you are doubly lucky. I saw Rigoletto a few nights ago. Gavelli gives quite the performance."

Hester and Lucy exchanged a glance, and Lucy was suddenly transported back to middle school—a girl with the earliest rumblings of a schoolgirl crush.

"What about those of us who aren't big opera fans?" Oscar asked, groaning. "Will I make it through it without falling asleep, or wanting to rip my ears out?"

Carrie rolled her eyes. "A little culture wouldn't hurt you, Oscar."

Lucy watched for Hester's reaction. She found her staring at Oscar like someone might look at their new puppy when he's just peed on the floor. Naughty, but still so adorable you have no choice but to forgive him.

"Before I go," Anna said, her eyes on the calendar app on her phone. "I have to move our tour of the Doge's Palace." Lucy took out her phone and notebook, and the two women found a time near the end of their weeks in Venice for a tour of the *palazzo* where the Venetian rulers had lived centuries ago. The marble building next door to the basilica reminded Lucy of a pink and white pastry confection.

Anna stood to leave and said her good-byes until the next day when they would be taking a walking tour of the city. As she started to walk away, Hester followed her for a few steps before stopping Anna and having a quiet conversation out of the earshot of the rest of the crew.

When Hester returned to the table, she was grinning. "Okay, everyone, what shall we do for lunch today?"

After a quick discussion, it was decided that Oscar would go his own way for the next two hours. He told them he wanted a chance to meander through the city to get a general feel for the place and that he'd grab a slice of pizza or something along the way. Lucy knew, however, that he was going in search of a studio where he might be able to enhance the image from Burano. Before leaving for St. Mark's, he'd shown her what he'd accomplished the night before. While it was clearer, it was still impossible to see any identifying features.

The three women would also find a quick bite after heading out with Hester on a mysterious errand—one she wasn't ready to divulge. Though Lucy had a good idea what it was.

Lucy chuckled to herself. It was only day three in Venice and already the little group was dealing in secretive missions of their own.

And all because Lucy couldn't walk away from Aurelia's murder.

If ever there had been an incentive for Lucy to renew her gym membership, Venice was it. As she and Carrie followed Hester through the city and across its many bridges culminating in the Accademia bridge that crossed the Grand Canal, Lucy cursed herself. Every muscle in her legs cried out for mercy. Fortunately, some clouds had moved in since they were sitting in the square, so her sweating was kept to a minimum.

Not far from the other side of the bridge Hester stopped, a wide grin on her face. She gazed up at the impressive white facade. Lucy followed her gaze and found the words, *Accademia Di Belle Arti,* at the very top.

"Ah, the Accademia art museum," Lucy said, pleased she had done her research on the many museums in Venice.

"Indeed," Hester said in a reverent whisper. "My favorite art history professor is now working here, and she's agreed to meet us to talk about…" She paused and quickly surveyed the area near them. Then, lowering her voice again, she continued, "the painting."

Carrie and Lucy nodded knowingly.

Throughout their trek across the city, Lucy had wondered if she should tell Hester that she was wearing her cardigan inside out. Now that she knew whom they would be meeting, she decided it best to let her know.

"Uh, Hester sweetie, your sweater is inside out."

Flustered, Hester pulled the bright blue sweater off and tried to turn it right side out. However, this seemed to be a Herculean task as first one sleeve then the other didn't behave as she was trying to make it.

Lucy sighed and grabbed the sweater from her friend, adjusted it, and handed it back.

"Thank you," Hester said. "You know me and my…"

She left the rest unsaid as Lucy knew only too well.

With the cardigan properly in place, the three women joined the line leading into the museum. It moved slowly, but ten minutes later they were purchasing tickets and stepping into the famous museum.

Inside, Lucy found the entrance foyer rather plain and uninspired. But she knew, from her research, that the rooms throughout were each splendid in their own, individual ways.

While Carrie and Lucy waited in the center of the room, Hester went over to one of the counters where visitors could get information on the museum and spoke to the young woman manning the counter.

A minute later Hester rejoined them. "Caterina will be joining us in just a moment." Lucy noted the energy shooting off Hester. Her blue eyes were brighter than normal. "You'll love her. She has this remarkable way of making anyone fall in love with art. Caterina changed my entire perspective on art and is the reason I went on and got the master's in art history."

After such an intro, Lucy suspected it would be difficult for the woman to live up to the hype.

An elegant Italian woman in her late fifties or early sixties strode toward their group. At least as tall as Hester and dressed in a smart gray suit and white silk blouse with a bold silver necklace at her throat, the woman wore her voluminous salt and pepper hair in a swept back, layered, chin-length style that Lucy found herself coveting. Lucy self-consciously touched her own boring hair that had decided to be uncooperative that morning.

As Caterina stepped up to them, Lucy made a point to stand straighter when she noted Caterina's perfect posture.

"*Buongiorno,*" she greeted Hester, as she kissed her cheek. Hester returned the gesture.

"Caterina, I'd like you to meet my friends, Lucy and Carrie."

After all of the niceties had been tended to, Caterina said, "Let us go back to my office where we can speak without fear of being overheard."

Lucy realized that Hester must have given her some idea of why she had asked for the meeting.

They followed Caterina down a hallway to an office on the outside wall that enjoyed a large window with a view out onto the *campo*. The office walls were covered with paintings from every era, up through modern abstract art. Lucy hoped they were only *reproductions* of the paintings. Something told her, however, that these were not reproductions.

"Please, sit and make yourselves comfortable."

The large office had a grouping of a love seat and two easy chairs in one corner. Once everyone was seated, Caterina said, "So, I understand you have some questions about a painting you have happened upon."

"We do," Hester said. "And it is of the utmost importance that this be kept confidential, as it might be part of a police investigation."

This news appeared to alarm Caterina as she adjusted her already straight back and began to frown.

"Hester, I have concerns about becoming involved in something illegal."

"No, no, you won't be. I simply want your opinion on a painting we found. I've taken several photos, but they are only on my phone and the lighting wasn't ideal so the images aren't as good as I'd have liked. But I think you'll be able to see enough to be able to tell us something about it."

Caterina looked from Hester, who sat next to her on the love seat, to Lucy and finally to Carrie, making eye contact with each.

She gave a curt nod. "Show me."

"I transferred them to my iPad so they could be seen in a larger format," Hester explained as she removed the tablet from her large purse. Although she could easily afford purses from any of the high-end lines, Lucy knew she preferred the inexpensive department store purses. This aqua colored leather satchel was one of her favorites.

Three taps on the screen later she held up the tablet for Caterina to inspect.

Lucy carefully observed Caterina's reactions. First, Caterina's eyes became huge, then she closed them, breathing in through her nose, her shoulders lifting as she inhaled.

When she opened them again, she took the iPad from Hester and zoomed in on sections of the photograph. Her lips went through a series of gymnastic moves as she inspected the picture.

"Where did you find this?"

"I'm sorry, Caterina, I can't tell you. Yet," Hester told her.

This earned Hester a deep scowl before Caterina said, "It appears to be a long-lost Canaletto. Whether it is or is not can only be determined upon closer inspection of the actual painting."

"Is it the one thought to be stolen by the Nazi's?" Lucy asked.

"If it is authentic, it would appear to be."

"Does it look like his painting, *Piazza Santa Margherita*?" Hester asked in a reverent whisper.

Caterina nodded as she stared at the image on the tablet.

"You know, don't you, that should this turn out to be the genuine painting, it would be the find of the decade, if not century?" Caterina asked the group.

They all voiced their understanding of its importance.

Lucy leaned forward. "So, *if* this turns out to be the real McCoy, how do you think it might have found itself in a home in Venice?"

"I'm sorry, real McCoy?"

"The genuine article. The real missing Canaletto painting."

Lucy could see Caterina consider the question and was careful to allow her time to think it through. Carrie and Hester, too, remained silent.

Finally, Caterina said, "It is impossible to say."

Lucy's shoulders slumped and she lowered her head to the level of her chest.

"However..." Caterina said, causing Lucy to sit up straight and fix her eyes on the art historian. "Let me ask a question. Do you know if this is a Venetian home that has been in the family for more than a generation?"

Lucy answered. "We've been told that it's been in the family for multiple generations."

This sent Caterina's head nodding.

"Then it is possible that a family member during the war years had a connection to the German Nazis. Or perhaps a connection to someone within Germany who had knowledge of the locations where the art was warehoused. They might have been paid off with a painting for some favor they did. Or…"

She pursed her lips and thought for a few beats.

"It is also quite possible that this came to the family much more recently. It could have been discovered and stolen. The possibilities are rather endless, I'm afraid."

Lucy opened her mouth to ask a question when Caterina beat her to it.

"Is it possible for you to describe how the painting was hidden? What I hope to hear is if it was packed in something."

Hester answered. "It was in a wooden packing crate. Inside the crate, it was wrapped in an old blanket."

One corner of Caterina's mouth went up. "Ahhh…did the crate appear old? Did the wood have an old patina to it?"

Lucy and Hester looked to one another as they tried to see the crate in their minds' eyes.

"It seemed old to me," Lucy said. "The nails that I had to remove were definitely old and a little rusty."

"And the blanket. Hester, you said it was an old blanket. How could you tell that?"

"It was one of those old woolen blankets without any discernible color. Very plain, unadorned. Utilitarian."

"In other words very much like the blankets issued to soldiers during the war," Caterina said.

Hester and Lucy exchanged another look.

"But I didn't see any tags or lettering on it that would have identified it as belonging to someone's army." It disappointed Lucy to have to say it.

"I don't think that much would have still been visible," Caterina said. "And you probably weren't looking for any markings at the time."

Lucy slapped her thigh. "Right! I didn't. I mean, here was this old painting inside it—the blanket was of zero interest at that point."

"Exactly," Caterina said.

"What should we do now?" Hester asked her beloved professor.

"Nothing. Not until the police can do their part. The last thing you want is to have the police looking for you." She took a perfectly manicured finger and pointed it at each of the three women in turn. "However, you can send me all the pictures you took, and I can see if there's anything I can do at this end."

That news cheered Lucy and Hester.

They all stood and thanked Caterina for her time and help.

"Ah, but before you leave, would you not like to see a true Canaletto?" She smiled devilishly and cocked a brow.

Hester clapped her hands once. "Of course, Signora Caterina!"

Lucy didn't waste any time getting on board for this one, thinking that seeing the real thing in real life would help her weigh the chances that the one they had found was authentic or not.

Like a mother duck leading her ducklings, Caterina led the way through the many floors, rooms, and corridors until they arrived at the room where the Canaletto was displayed.

Once they stepped into the room, their pace slowed. Only a handful of other visitors were in the room, and none of them were in front of the painting they were interested in.

Lucy shivered as she gazed at *Return of the Bucintoro to the Molo on Ascension Day.*

Painted from a perspective across the Grand Canal from the Doge's Palace and Piazza San Marco, it showed not only the palace and entry to the *piazza*, but the chaotic boat traffic on the canal.

Lucy let a soft laugh erupt.

"It could have been painted today. All those boats going this way and that. No different from today. Not to mention the palace, and setting, and...the life!"

"And that, Lucy," Caterina said with a hand on Lucy's shoulder, "is the genius of Canaletto. And the glory that is our unchanging Venice."

~ ten ~

AFTER A QUICK LUNCH OF pizza in a tiny eatery not far from the opera house, the three women moseyed through several *calli* and window shopped while they waited for their meeting time of one o'clock. Carrie and Lucy had gotten a ways ahead of Hester in one *calle* and stopped to laugh at paintings of cats dressed up in Renaissance finery in one shop window.

"Not exactly what you'd see at the Accademia, is it?" Lucy said with a snort. Her brief introduction into the fine arts had left her wanting to learn more. Even without any formal art education, she knew that cats in Renaissance clothing weren't considered a serious art form.

"Ohhh, look at those!" Hester said over Lucy and Carrie's shoulders when she'd caught up to them. "Aren't they so adorable! I want one."

Lucy and Carrie turned to face their friend, shock and horror on their faces.

"Really?" Lucy snarled.

"Oh yes." Hester's eyes beamed with joy.

"You're kidding, right?" Lucy tried again. "You're the one with the degree in art history from Oxford. Have you lost your mind?"

Hester stuck her nose in the air and started for the shop door. "No, I have not lost my mind," she said over her shoulder.

Hester's two bewildered friends followed her into the shop and watched in a state of stupefaction as she purchased a print of a tabby cat wearing a tricorne hat with three massive ostrich plumes coming from the center, a Tudor ruff at its neck, and a highly embellished fur cape over a heavily embroidered vest covered in regal medals. The ghastly picture was framed in a large, garish, gilt frame.

Once the picture was carefully wrapped in bubble-wrap and paper, its new owner skipped out into the *calle*, followed at a safe distance by her shocked friends.

Lucy eventually hurried to Hester's side, her curiosity getting the better of her.

"Hester, honey. Can you explain to me why an art aficionado like yourself would buy such a ridiculous picture?"

Hester smiled at Lucy. "Because it makes me happy. Who couldn't smile when they see something like this?" She tapped the bundle she carried under her arm. "Not all art is high art. Some is simply there to make us happy. This cat makes me happy."

Lucy took a deep breath, and as she let it out slowly, she thought about how Hester's answer summed up the woman in a nutshell. Yes, she was brilliant. Beautiful. Eccentric. Kind to a fault. But she also had never lost her childlike enthusiasm for life. It didn't matter if everyone appreciated cat paintings or not—if she saw one that made her happy she would buy it.

Lucy wished she could embrace even a small amount of Hester's joy for life. She recognized the fact that she was too cynical to become a Hester. But perhaps that cynicism was self-imposed. Brought on by the past several years of life.

She looked at her beaming best friend and gave her a smile.

"Well, I can see it makes you very happy."

"Yep," Hester sang.

As they turned down another *calle,* Lucy felt the icy sensation she equated with being watched. She turned and scanned the throng of shopping tourists behind her. No one stood out from the crowd, and she tried to convince herself that it was nothing, but as soon as she continued on a few more steps, the sensation returned.

She began a mental conversation with herself. Who would be following or watching her? No one in Venice knew her, so no one would have reason to keep her under surveillance. She eventually convinced herself that her imagination had run away with her.

Due to all of Lucy's stopping for imaginary spies, Hester and Carrie had managed to get twenty-five yards ahead of her. An advertisement in one shop window caught her attention, and she ducked into the establishment.

Five minutes later she stepped back into the *calle* with a new lilt in her step.

She hurried down the *calle* in search of her friends, whom

she finally found standing along a wall, waiting for her.

"Where've you been?" Carrie barked at her.

"Excuse me, Carrie," Lucy snapped back. Then with a deep breath in an effort to return to a state of equanimity, she said, "I stopped to look at something. Then I couldn't make my way through the crowd." To illustrate her lie she waved an arm at the mass of people clogging the narrow throughway. "And thank you for waiting for me."

Hester patted her on the arm. "Of course, Lucy. Now I think we should make our way to La Fenice."

"About that…" Lucy said. "I need to take care of something. It shouldn't take more than a few hours, but I'm going to have to miss the tour of the opera house. I'll see it when we go to the opera, anyway. Take lots of notes and make sure Oscar takes plenty of pictures."

"You sleuthing?" Carrie asked, clearly suspicious.

Lucy smirked. "Maybe…"

"We'll take care of everything at the opera house," Hester assured her with a smile. "You do whatever you need to do."

"Thanks. I've gotta run."

Lucy turned, and without another word headed back the way she had come.

She would need every minute of those few hours.

An hour and a half later Lucy stepped out of a shop feeling as if she'd been through a surgical procedure. One with no anesthetic.

Each time she blinked, massive caterpillars obscured her

view. How was she supposed to find her way to the next shop she'd been directed to, with caterpillars in her eyes?

She had never before worn false eyelashes. And she couldn't understand why anyone would want to go through life with caterpillars stuck to their eyelids.

As she glanced at her reflection in a shop window her normally mousey, dull hair was unrecognizable. It now had a definite Italian flair to it. Or perhaps it was a 'just-got-out-of-bed' style. Cut short in the back but with long floppy layers in front, it went this way and that. And it was now more red than mousey brown. Red and gold highlights had been added, but to Lucy's eye all she could see was red. Lucille Ball red. Though she suspected that she was imagining such a vibrant red. At least she hoped she was.

Her makeover girl had sent her to a clothing boutique that she promised would complete her transformation. If the salespeople in the boutique could keep from laughing themselves to death, they would quickly peg her as an easy mark. With the navy capris and white blouse, she wore orthopedic sandals. Anything they dressed her in would be an improvement.

Two hours later Lucy exited the boutique carrying three large bags of purchases while she teetered on high-heeled strappy sandals in which she was expected to navigate the cobblestones. She wore an above the knee striped pencil skirt and a white, silk T-shirt. The fact that she somehow appeared to be ten pounds slimmer was owed to the torturous foundation garment the saleswoman assured her she needed. Would enjoy. Would change her life.

Yes, Lucy thought, *if I ever decide to give up the ability to breathe then this weapon of torture would be exactly what I would want.*

But she knew she would be wearing it when she went to see Nicolo perform at La Fenice. And the dress she'd be wearing was neatly wrapped in tissue paper and lay in one of the three bags.

Lucy shut her hotel room door behind her, dropped her bags, and reached down to remove the instruments of torture attached to her feet. Despite the throbbing sensation still present, she could almost hear her feet singing out their gratitude for their freedom.

She slowly made her way to the bed. There was nothing she wanted more in the world than to fling herself onto it. But she needed to keep her look together for when she met up with Hester, Carrie, and Oscar. She'd received a text from Hester that they'd be back at four o'clock and to meet them at the sidewalk cafe next to the hotel. That gave her ten minutes to rest. Ever so carefully she lay down, making sure she didn't wrinkle her clothes or muss her hair in any way. She couldn't wait to see their faces when they first laid eyes on her new look.

While she gave her pained body a short rest, she opened her phone to the photos she'd taken in Aurelia's apartment. She was most interested in the pictures of the address book.

It appeared that Aurelia had organized the entries by first name, rather than by the more customary method of alphabetizing by last name.

On the second page, she zoomed in on one particular entry that looked different than the others. First, it was apparent that this entry had been written over another that had been erased. The information was now written in blue ink, and when compared to other names and addresses written in blue ink, this one showed little if any fading.

But it was the way she'd written the name that stood out. There was no first and last name, only initials. A. O. There was no address, but instead what was written looked like a place name or business name. She'd need Hester to translate for her. And finally, there was no phone number.

Lucy noticed the time at the top of the phone screen. 3:59. Time for her grand entrance. She forced her weary body to stand, and hobbled over to where she'd left her shoes. With tears threatening to well up in her eyes she stared at the sexy, but painful shoes.

On they went. Though the screams coming from her feet could probably be heard throughout the hotel.

A quick glance in the bathroom mirror reassured Lucy that the caterpillars were still in place and her hair looked no more or less mussed than before her brief rest.

With her purse in the crook of her elbow and her hand held fashionably up, Lucy sashayed out of the room, a wiggle in her hips and sheer, intense pain coming from her feet.

Lucy saw her group sitting at a table, chatting, before they saw her. With as much grace as she could muster she made her way over the paving stones and to their table.

She stood next to the table, shoulders squared, spine straight, head held high, waiting to be noticed.

Carrie was the first to glance up at her. Then she looked away, ready to continue her conversation with Hester and Oscar. A split second later her head flew around, eyes bulging, mouth hanging open.

"Lucy?" Carrie wailed.

Hester and Oscar followed Carrie's gaze and looked up at the New and Improved Lucy Tuppence.

"What. Is. This?" Carrie asked, waving a hand up and down in Lucy's direction.

Lucy saw Oscar trying to hold in a laugh. Hester's look of shock was slowly turning into a grin.

Keeping her head held high, Lucy answered Carrie. "This is European Lucy. A confident, stylish woman about town, Lucy Tuppence."

Carrie giggled. "Okay, if you say so."

"Well, I for one, love it," Hester said, cheering Lucy. "It never hurts to try new things. You look lovely, Lucy."

"Thank you, Hester." She shot a glare at the traitor Carrie.

Lucy grabbed a chair and pulled it out. "But for the love of God, I need to sit! These shoes should be outlawed."

Forgetting any thought of grace for the moment, Lucy fell into the chair with a loud sigh.

"That's the price of glamour," Carrie said with a laugh and a snort.

For the next twenty minutes, Lucy listened to tales of Teatro La Fenice while she flipped through photographs of the famous opera house on Oscar's iPad. He'd thoughtfully downloaded to his iPad everything he'd taken.

"It's spectacular," Lucy whispered, in awe. Oscar's pictures showed a theater dripping in elegance and opulence. She could imagine sitting in the theater watching and listening to Nicolo performing. *Soon,* she thought.

"You know," Hester began, "for a building that has burned down more than once, the name *The Phoenix* is certainly appropriate. It has truly risen from the ashes."

A waiter brought espressos and small Italian pastries to the table. "We went ahead and ordered for you," Oscar explained to Lucy. "Hope you don't mind."

Lucy's mouth watered as she admired the delicately decorated chocolate pastry that had been placed before her. Italy was going to be the undoing of her perpetual diet.

"No, not at all," she said, almost drooling.

"Yum…" Carrie said with a sigh.

"Hey, Hester, I'm hoping you can translate something for me," Lucy said, bringing out her phone. She opened to the photo of the page with the curious entry and zoomed in. "This is from Aurelia's address book. I think it could mean something. What does that say?" She handed the phone to Hester.

Hester peered at it. "Bonomini and Malfante Accountants. It looks like an accounting firm."

Lucy took the phone back and entered the business name into her search engine. A moment later she had an address. She put the address into Google maps and got a location. After a minute of analysis and much zooming in and out she determined it wasn't far from where she was.

Hester, who had been watching all of this, asked Lucy,

"Would you like me to come with you? That is, if you're planning on going there now?"

Lucy gave her a withering look. "Only if I plan to communicate with them." When Hester didn't pick up on the heavy sarcasm, Lucy added, "Yes, Hester. I'll need you."

"And what are Oscar and I supposed to be doing while you two go out playing Venetian snoops."

"I think you mean, *sleuths*, Carrie," Lucy snapped.

Carrie shook her head. "No, I meant snoops."

Lucy pulled out the big notebook with all of the filming and research plans and flipped to a tab.

"Tomorrow we have the walking tour of Venice," she said to Carrie and Oscar, handing them a map covered with highlighter markings. "We'll have our guide, but perhaps it would be a good idea for you two to scope it out a bit today. This shows the areas, *campi*, and *calli* we're doing. Oscar, you know the drill, figure out how you'll want to film everything. Carrie, decide where you should stand for your parts. And I'm really sorry I'm abandoning you so much. It's just that I can't let this Aurelia thing go."

"Yeah, we noticed," Oscar grumbled. Lucy turned to check Hester's reaction to his comment, but all she could see was the glowing appreciation for all that was Oscar and every utterance he made. Being with him on a daily basis was having an effect on Hester. Lucy wasn't certain the effect was a good thing.

"I'll make it up to you, I promise."

"You know what?" Carrie said cheerfully. "It's a gorgeous afternoon, and we've been indoors for a while. I'm looking forward to walking about Venice."

Lucy gave her a smile and nodded.

"Okay, then stay in touch via text messages. We'll meet up later. Maybe," Lucy said.

Then, turning to Hester, she said, "Off to Campo San Bartolomeo. I need a good accountant."

As she stood to leave, the only hitch in her plan that reared its ugly head shouted at her from the stones beneath her feet.

Her feet and those dang shoes.

Suck it up, Buttercup, she admonished herself. *This is the look someone looking for an accountant needs.*

She'd taken five steps before wondering once again how the European women did it.

~ eleven ~

AMPO SAN BARTOLOMEO WAS A small but busy square, with a large monument in the center, topped with a statue to someone who seemed to have stepped out of the 1600's.

Lucy and Hester walked the perimeter of the *campo*, searching for the building that housed the Bonomini and Malfante Accountants. They discovered it near the monument. It was on the floor directly above a small shop.

They found the stairs and made their way to the first floor and the door with the Bonomini and Malfante Accountants plaque next to it. There was another sign next to it with what Lucy assumed were the names of the accountants associated with the firm. She scanned the list of six names, and only one matched the initials in Aurelia's address book.

Alberti Oliveto.

Limping a bit, Lucy walked in and smiled broadly at the receptionist.

"*Buongiorno. Mi scusi,* do you speak English?" Lucy asked.

Without so much as a glimmer of a smile, the receptionist shook her head sharply.

Hester stepped in. After a minute of Italian back and forth, Hester turned to Lucy. "She says that if we wait for a few minutes, Mr. Oliveto can give us two or three minutes of his very valuable time."

Without taking her eyes off the receptionist, Lucy smiled and said, "Fine. We shall sit and wait."

As she sat down on one of the few chairs in the small waiting area, Lucy worried that she might not be able to get back up. She wondered if it would have been better to remain standing. Feet only swell when you sit.

Luckily for Lucy's feet, Mr. Oliveto didn't keep them waiting long. They were shown to his tiny office.

Alberti Oliveto was in his early fifties, was about Hester's height, and still sported a full head of dark hair that he quite obviously dyed. The pinkie on his right hand sported a gaudy lump of gold with a large diamond in the center. Lucy held strong opinions about the kind of men who wore pinkie rings, especially oversized gold ones with diamonds. She didn't care for them.

Hester took the lead. Lucy listened as Hester spun the tale they'd agreed upon on the walk over to the *campo*. Hester was purchasing a second home in Venice and would require accounting services. An acquaintance had mentioned his name. The acquaintance was Aurelia Carotti.

Throughout Hester's spiel, Lucy watched Oliveto's face. When Hester mentioned Aurelia's name, Lucy was sure she hadn't imagined him flinching ever so slightly.

He began to shake his head.

"I do not recall anyone by that name."

Lucy said, "Maybe you didn't know her surname. Perhaps you knew her by her maiden name. Could you have done her family's accounting? A family with an Aurelia?" She wished she had thought to find out what her maiden name had been. "Did you know an Aurelia?"

Oliveto narrowed his eyes as he considered the questions. Finally, he nodded slowly.

"It could sound familiar. I might have met an Aurelia, but it isn't an uncommon name." He shrugged. "I wouldn't be able to say if it was the same person. If I ever knew a woman by that name."

"Just a moment," Lucy said. "I need to confer with my friend." She led Hester closer to the door.

"You know…" Lucy began, whispering behind a hand, an idea forming in her mind. "If she was planning to unload what we found, maybe she was going to have him hide the money in a Cayman Island account or something. There's no way he would be truthful about knowing her."

Hester whispered back, "And she wouldn't have written his name in her book."

"Exactly!" Lucy said it aloud. She took the three steps back to the desk, Hester following her. "Thank you for your time. We think that you might not be the accountant our friend recommended."

A look of relief quickly passed over his face.

The two women left the office as quickly as Lucy could hobble out of there.

Back in the *campo*, Lucy went over to the monument, perched alongside it, removed one sandal, and massaged the foot.

"He definitely knows something. He flinched when you first mentioned Aurelia's name. No question about it. I think he was going to do a little off-the-books accounting for her."

Now that Lucy's head was at the level of Hester's thigh, she noticed a large marinara stain on her left pant leg. Too bad Hester hadn't chosen to wear something red that day.

"That sounds quite possible." Hester said it like she was commenting on the probability of a mutation in a cell division experiment.

"You know, that didn't take very long," Lucy said. "Maybe we could swing by Aurelia's apartment—see if the roommate is in."

"It's a bit of a walk," Hester gently pointed out, her eyes on the foot receiving the impromptu massage.

"Yeah," Lucy conceded. Her eyes scanned the shops around the square. If she was lucky, perhaps someone sold some flat sandals. Or sneakers. Or orthopedic shoes.

Lucy would have taken anything at that moment.

Seeing nothing, she put the high-heeled sandal back on her foot, stood up tall, and moved with the wiggle in her hips, even if her walk was more of a hobble.

Hester pointed the way, and the two started off toward Aurelia's.

Only five minutes into the hike, Lucy shouted, "Hold it!" and disappeared into a shop. Hester loitered outside, waiting for her friend. While she waited, she was whistled at no fewer than three times.

When Lucy reappeared, she was stuffing the high heels into her large purse. She walked with a skip in her step.

On her feet, she wore black Converse high-tops.

Perhaps it wasn't the fashion statement she hoped to make, but it certainly was some kind of fashion statement.

While standing in front of Aurelia's door, Lucy switched back to the heels. She felt the need to make the proper impression on the roommate.

Once she was properly shod, she knocked on the door, hoping it would be answered this time.

They didn't have to wait long. A slender woman in her forties wearing skinny jeans and a peach-colored tunic opened the door. Her long salt and pepper hair was pulled back in a loose ponytail. She looked wary as she eyed Lucy and Hester.

"*Buongiorno,*" Lucy said with a friendly smile. Then she turned it over to Hester, whom she assumed was introducing the two of them and giving a believable reason for their visit.

When Hester finished speaking, the roommate opened the door wide and invited them in.

"Your Italian is excellent," she said, "but I speak English if you prefer."

"Well, I do," Lucy said. "You just heard the extent of my Italian."

This brought the first small smile from the woman. Lucy

noted the red-rimmed eyes and dark circles beneath them.

"My name is Laura. Laura Bacci. I'm Aurelia's roommate. Or I was her roommate." Lucy heard a catch in Laura's voice. "How did you say you knew Aurelia?"

"We were there when her body was found in the canal," Lucy explained, her voice soft and serious.

"Oh how horrible for you." Laura covered her mouth with a hand.

"You see, I have a background in law enforcement, and I feel as if I owe it to Aurelia, since I was there at the canal, to help find her killer. We're hoping you can share anything about Aurelia's life that might help me with solving her murder."

"Oh...I see. Well, please sit down. We can talk." She motioned to the sofa in the living room, and Lucy and Hester sat while Laura sat across from them.

"Aurelia, she was a good, good woman." Laura held her hands tightly clasped in her lap. A deep furrow appeared between her eyes. "But she had terrible luck choosing men."

Lucy nodded, understanding only too well. Hester's face was unchanged, having little experience in this area.

"I know she was separated from her husband," Lucy said.

"Yes, that no good Enzo. He made her life miserable. But she left him, oh, it must be about eight or nine months ago. Then she started seeing Lorenzo. They met through friends. She was over the moon in love with him. But me, I got a strange feeling about him. Not so sure. You know?"

Lucy told Laura she understood exactly what she meant.

"Do you think either of them would harm Aurelia?" Hester asked.

They watched as Laura considered this question.

A moment later, she said, "Enzo, yes. I can imagine that. He has a temper. Especially when he's been drinking. Lorenzo? I don't think so. But you never know. There was that strange feeling I had about him."

"Do you know of anyone else who might have wanted to kill her?" Lucy asked.

Laura shook her head. "No. Like I said, Aurelia was a good woman."

Lucy watched as tears formed in the corners of Laura's eyes.

"I'm so sorry for your loss," Lucy said. "I know you'll miss her."

Hester also extended her condolences. She and Lucy stood.

"Do you happen to know where we might find Lorenzo?" Lucy asked.

Laura glanced at her watch. She still wore a watch in the day of the ubiquitous phone, and Lucy wondered if it was a European thing or just Laura.

"At this hour he's usually downstairs at the bar meeting up with his father for a drink. Lorenzo is a good son. Keeps his eye on his elderly father."

"Well, that's nice of him," Lucy said. "Maybe he's a good guy after all."

Laura made a shrugging motion that Lucy recognized from Italian movies. She thought it meant, 'meh.'

"You know," Laura said to Lucy. "You don't look American. You have excellent style, Lucy. I love those sandals. And your hair. *Magnifico!*"

Lucy beamed, even as her feet felt betrayed. "Thank you. I try." No need to tell her the look was only hours old.

"How will we recognize Lorenzo?" Hester asked. Lucy could see she was fighting off a laugh.

"Tall. Skinny. Roman nose. In his forties. Probably sitting with an old man."

Hester giggled. "Oh yeah. His father. Of course. That should be easy."

They thanked Laura, again offered their condolences, and left to find Lorenzo The Boyfriend.

There were fewer than a dozen patrons in the bar when the two women walked in.

Lucy felt every eye in the room turn to them. Normally it was the tall, gorgeous blonde she was with who got all of the attention, but on this occasion she sensed that she, too, was the object of some interest. She stood a little taller.

A quick survey of the small room didn't turn up any men in their forties sitting with an elderly man, but there was one man sitting alone who matched Laura's description of Lorenzo. Lucy led the way over to his table.

The man leaned one elbow on the table, his head resting in the hand. His full attention was on the coaster he played with, spinning it on its side, over and over. He appeared despondent, as if he'd just lost his girlfriend.

"*Mi scusi,*" Lucy said quietly. The man looked up. "Lorenzo?"

His eyes darted from one woman to the other. Hester said something to him in Italian. He nodded.

"Yes, this is Lorenzo. He says to join him. I told him why we're here."

Lucy and Hester sat at the table.

"Ask him the usual questions. Like did he know anyone who would want to hurt Aurelia."

Hester relayed the question.

Lorenzo shook his head. "I think…" he began in halting English. "Aurelia, she did not tell me…something. Keep…something from me knowing."

"Do you have any idea what it could have been?" Lucy asked, carefully enunciating each word.

He looked to Hester, who quickly translated.

"No," he said, shaking his head. "But…it…bother Aurelia. Worried Aurelia."

"Something was worrying her? Did she seem afraid?"

Hester didn't wait for Lorenzo to ask for a translation this time, and repeated the questions in Italian.

He thought for a moment. "Worry, yes." He added something in Italian.

"No, she wasn't afraid," Hester told Lucy.

"Maybe she was worried about how she was going to turn the painting into money without getting caught," Lucy suggested.

Hester gave a little nod.

"*Grazie*, Lorenzo," Lucy said. "Please tell him how sorry I am about Aurelia."

After Hester said all of the right things, they got up to

leave. As they turned toward the door they saw an older man approaching the table. He had Lorenzo's nose, and despite a significant hunch in his shoulders, he was still rather tall. The two women smiled at him as they made for the exit.

Out in the bright daylight, Lucy felt the blast of the hot sun. The day had warmed significantly since lunchtime. It didn't take but a minute before she felt the tickle of a drop of sweat trying to make its way under her foundation garment. She looked around for a place to perch so she could at least change back into her Converses.

But before she could locate a perch, her attention was drawn to the outer door of Aurelia's flat. Two uniformed police officers led an ashen, handcuffed Laura out of the building. Despite the heels, Lucy hurried over to Laura.

As she approached, Lucy caught the glares the two officers shot at her. One was male, the other female, but the expressions on their faces were identical. They might as well have shouted at Lucy: Halt!

Not to be deterred, Lucy stopped a safe distance, and in a loud and clear voice, asked Laura, "What has happened? Why are they arresting you?"

Laura looked first to one officer, then the other, before turning toward Lucy. "They think I might have killed Aurelia! Which I didn't! And they think I stole some painting, which is, how do you say, insane!"

She didn't have the opportunity to say much more as they led her down a *calle*. Lucy mused on the idea of arrests in Venice. Did the arrested person have to walk all the way to the police headquarters? They certainly weren't put into cars. Or were they led to a nearby canal and put into a boat? Whichever it was, she felt sorry for Laura.

Hester stepped up next to Lucy. "She didn't murder anyone," Hester said. "And I'm sure she didn't even know about the Canaletto. They have the wrong person."

"I couldn't agree more. All the more reason for us to find the real murderer."

Having forgotten her miserable feet, Lucy began marching across the cobblestones in the general direction of their hotel. At least she hoped it was the right direction.

They hadn't gone far when Lucy noticed the same young man she'd seen in front of Aurelia's apartment the day before. As they passed him, Lucy's eyes met his. He didn't look away, as one would expect. The look made Lucy shiver. It felt threatening.

Was he watching them? And if he was, why?

Lucy hoped she would soon have that connection with the local police. She needed information. Not to mention some sense of protection. Though she knew enough to know that wouldn't be the case. Certainly not in a foreign country.

Still, it couldn't hurt, she thought to herself.

~ twelve ~

LUCY WAS LATE TO BREAKFAST on the hotel terrace, as it took her an inordinate amount of time to figure out how to apply her makeup and do her hair. After three tries at applying the caterpillar lashes, she decided to forego them. She didn't take long to chose what she would wear for the day, however. After yesterday, this day felt like a capris and blouse day. Worn with athletic shoes.

She joined the rest of the group, who were already halfway finished with their breakfast. Oscar was already returning to the buffet for seconds.

"You look nice this morning," Carrie said kindly. "Though Glamour Lucy was interesting."

Lucy forced herself to smile. "Glamour Lucy isn't gone. She's just going a little more casual today."

"Actually, I was going to ask you where you went for your makeover," Carrie said. "Maybe the clothing shop too, though they probably don't carry clothes for curvy people like me. Maybe they could direct me to someplace that does! I think it would be fun to try on a new look."

Lucy held in a laugh. Carrie tried on a new look almost weekly. New hair colors, including all the colors of the rainbow. New clothing styles. She was never one to let herself become predictable. Lucy admired that about Carrie.

Oscar returned to the table. As Carrie and Hester chatted about the walking tour, he leaned over to Lucy, who sat next to him.

"Got that matter taken care of," he whispered to her. "Won't tell you much, but you might see more. I can show you later today."

"Thank you. That would be great. And, Oscar, I was going to ask you if, after the walk, you could get some shots of Santa Maria Della Salute, both from the water and on land."

"Is that the massive church with the dome at the entrance to the Grand Canal?" Oscar asked as he wrote himself a reminder in a small notebook.

"Yep. Built by the Venetians in the 1600's after they made a deal with God. They would build a church to the Virgin Mary if he would end the plague. It had killed a third of Venice's population."

"Oh my God," Carrie wailed as she shivered. "A third? Wow."

"I know. Makes you glad you live in the twenty-first century, doesn't it?" Lucy said.

Leaving Carrie to her gloomy plague thoughts, Lucy got up to get some breakfast and a double espresso. With her plate filled with eggs and fruit, she gazed at the tray filled with brioche. Some had glistening bits of chocolate embedded within them. She debated the pros and cons of a chocolate brioche. Knowing the mileage she'd put in that day, she placed one on her plate.

The group was finishing up breakfast—Lucy still had a bite of the pastry sitting on her plate—when two police officers walked toward their table. A hush fell over the terrace as the tourists all turned their attention to the uniformed men. At least these, like the officers who took away Laura, were not Carabinieri with their intimidating military uniforms. These wore white uniform shirts and black trousers and could have been police officers just about anywhere in the world.

They stopped at Lucy's table. Four pairs of eyes stared up at the men.

Hester was about to act as Italian spokeswoman when one of the officers said, "Lucy Tuppence? Hester Nilsson?"

Lucy's mouth went dry, making speech difficult. "Yes?" she squeaked. "I'm Lucy."

Hester held up a hand. "And I'm Hester." Then Hester asked them something in Italian. Lucy assumed she was asking what they could do for them.

The answer came in English. "We would like you to come with us. You are wanted for questioning."

"Questioning regarding what?" Hester asked before Lucy had a chance to ask the same question.

The officer looked at Carrie and Oscar, giving each the full once-over before answering Hester. "The detective will explain this to you when you are at the *Questura*."

"What is a *questura*?" Lucy asked, her tone more strident

than it should have been under the circumstances.

"You would call it police headquarters," the officer doing all of the talking answered sharply. "Now, if you will come with us."

The officers each took one step backward. Lucy took this as an order to get up and get moving. So she did. As she got up she made eye contact with Carrie. She hoped Carrie would understand that her look meant 'help us if needed!'

Hester quickly followed Lucy's example, and the two women left the terrace with the officers following close behind them.

As they left, Lucy could hear Oscar shout, "Don't worry. We'll take care of this!"

Lucy glanced at Hester to gauge how she was handling this unexpected turn of events. What she saw was Hester's mouth turned up in a pleased half-smile.

She knew Hester wasn't thinking about what they were about to face. No, she was reveling in Oscar's promise of assistance, as if it had been a declaration of love.

The talkative officer held out his hand to assist Lucy out of the sleek, blue and white boat with the large *Polizia* emblazoned on the side. They had stopped at a dock that led to a large brick building. Over the door hung a blue sign that informed them that they had indeed arrived at the *Questura*.

The *Questura* wasn't located in the charming part of the city, but instead was situated at the far end of Venice that was connected to the mainland by a large bridge. Cars could drive in this small area of the island. Lucy was immediately struck by the stench of diesel fumes and the unpleasant roar of car engines. Two things that had been blissfully missing from her past several days.

The two women were led down the dock, through the door, and into the *Questura* itself. Lucy felt immediately at home. This could have been any police headquarters anywhere in the world.

After they cleared security, the officers walked them to a small elevator into which the four of them squeezed. No one spoke on the short trip up two floors. Lucy carefully avoided all eye contact.

Officer Talkative showed them into an office, stepped up to a desk, and spoke in Italian to the female officer manning the desk. She nodded and said something in return.

He then turned to Lucy and Hester and said, "He is ready for you. If you will follow me."

Lucy grabbed Hester's hand and held it tightly. They kept their hands clasped together as they followed the officer down a short hallway.

They were shown into a sterile office containing a faux-wood desk, desk chair, metal filing cabinet, and two metal chairs. The man sitting behind the desk stood as they entered. He was in his sixties, balding, and wore a suit and tie. Lucy pegged him for a detective.

"*Buongiorno,* please have a seat." His English was clear and precise despite a thick accent.

Hester and Lucy did as they were told. Each sat up straight and folded their hands in their laps, eyes directed at the man who had their fate in his hands.

"Which of you is Lucy Tuppence?"

"I am," she answered, quickly adding, "Sir."

He turned to Hester. "Then that would make you…" He looked down at a page of notes on the desk. "Hester Nilsson, yes?"

Hester nodded and said, "Yes, sir, that is me."

"I am *Capo Ispettore*, Chief Inspector Pietro Affini. I am investigating the death of Aurelia Carotti, and I received a call yesterday that I found most interesting and perplexing."

Lucy's heart threw in an extra beat or two.

Chief Inspector Affini paused, and Lucy knew it was for effect. She forced herself to stay still, going so far as making sure she didn't blink.

"You may wonder about the nature of that call, no?" Again a pause.

Hester took the bait. "Yes, I do wonder. What was it about?" Her voice was thin and sounded forced.

"It was from an art historian at the Accademia. She called to report two Americans who were asking about a painting."

Lucy swallowed so loudly she was sure the detective heard it.

Affini paused again, and Lucy was tempted to shake the man.

But neither woman responded. Lucy would wait him out however long it took.

Affini picked up a pen on his desk and tapped it on a short stack of paper.

"You see, this wasn't just any painting. No…it was one

that disappeared back in World War Two. Taken by the Nazis, but never recovered. These two women wanted some information on it."

He stared at each woman in turn, then stood, walked over to the filing cabinet and placed a paper in a file. He did so unhurriedly. Lucy recognized the move as another maneuver to ratchet up their discomfort.

It was working.

She couldn't imagine that Hester's mentor, Caterina, would have had anything to do with putting them in this situation. Had she spoken to someone who in turn alerted the authorities?

"I believe these two women to be the two of you, Ms. Tuppence and Ms. Nilsson. Am I incorrect?"

Lucy found herself wishing she had an attorney with her.

She scooted forward in her chair. "Hester and I did go in to speak with Hester's friend, Caterina Berrini. We may have spoken in the broadest terms about paintings by Italian artists."

Affini leaned back in his chair. "Hmmm, that is most interesting. Why would two American women want to know about this?"

"I was an art history major at Oxford," Hester said. Lucy was impressed by the level tone with which she spoke. "I wanted to see Caterina while in Venice."

"Ahh, Ms. Nilsson, now that makes perfect sense." He gave her a wry smile. "But why did you ask about the Canaletto?" He feigned a casual, non-legal, interest.

Lucy looked at Hester, weighing their options.

"Look," Lucy said with authority. She was finished

pussyfooting around. "I know that you know exactly what happened, so why are we all taking part in this little charade? Yes, we asked about the Canaletto. We asked because we had learned that there might have been one in Aurelia Carotti's flat. Hester thought it might be the missing Canaletto, since she knows *a lot* about art history."

Affini nodded slowly, as he tapped the pen on the paper in a cadence that matched his nods.

"This is interesting, yes. But...how did you come to know about this painting in the murder victim's home?"

Lucy had a sudden vision of a grubby, dark cell in an Italian prison.

At least if she were to spend the rest of her days in an Italian prison cell, she would never again have to worry about fashion, make-up, and hairstyles.

Lucy narrowed her eyes at the detective. She gave him a laser stare as she spoke. "We went to the flat to talk to Aurelia's roommate. The door was open. The roommate was nowhere to be seen. We went in. I was concerned that perhaps something had happened to the roommate as well. I have a background in law enforcement. It was a natural concern to have. Under the circumstances. In checking out the place to reassure myself that the roommate wasn't in trouble I came across the painting."

One corner of Affini's mouth went up. "Ahh, finally, we have something close to the truth. Yes, you were in the flat. You found the painting. And you opened the crate it was in, did you not?"

Lucy didn't answer as visions of that Italian prison swam

in front of her. Hester remained silent.

"Why? Why would you open a wooden crate? Certainly, you did not think that the missing roommate was in the crate."

"Chief Inspector Affini, as I'm sure you know from the reports from the crime scene, I was one of the first people to come across Aurelia in the canal. As I said, I have a background in law enforcement, and it was with an interest in the murder that I went to talk to her roommate. When she didn't seem to be there, I searched the apartment to make sure she wasn't dead in a corner somewhere. When I opened Aurelia's closet, I saw the crate and was intrigued. It was wrong of me to open it. But I assure you it was with no illegal intentions that I did so."

Affini opened a file folder and flipped through some papers, finally pulling one out. He carefully examined it.

Then he turned his attention back to Lucy and Hester.

"I assume that even in the United States it is illegal to trespass, to interfere with an investigation, to open crates that do not belong to you."

As this wasn't a question, Lucy felt no compunction to answer.

"I see that one of my assistants looked into you and your background, Ms. Tuppence. You seem to be free of any criminal behavior. And I will allow you and your friend to go. *This time.* But you must understand that what you did was illegal in this country. No more illegal entry. No opening things that do not belong to you."

Lucy waited to say anything in answer. She expected

more. Perhaps something about interfering with his investigation. But, when several seconds passed without a word, she said, "Thank you, Chief Inspector Affini. Hester and I appreciate your generosity under the circumstances."

A knock on the office door kept Affini from answering.

The door opened, and a uniformed woman stepped in. She said something in Italian to which Affini answered with a nod. She left without another word.

Finishing their conversation, Affini said, "Just make sure we don't meet like this again."

"Thank you, Chief Inspector Affini," Hester said, her head bowed.

"Uh, before we leave," Lucy said, knowing that she was about to tread on dangerous ground. "About that painting. Would there be some way for us to find out if it turns out to be the true Canaletto that's been missing for seventy years?"

Affini made a sharp, laughing sound.

"Americans. You are a curious people. And pushy, I would say." His eyes met Lucy's. "But, I don't think any harm could come from you knowing the outcome of that testing."

"Thank you!" Lucy said a tad too loudly. Now he would add *loud* to the list of American attributes. Though she knew that every European already believed Americans were too loud and noisy.

"My colleague who just stepped in had a message for you two. She said that Deputy Inspector Maria Lazzara wishes to see you before you leave the Questura. She is also working on the Aurelia Carotti case. The officer at the desk outside my office can show you the way."

Lucy's heart dropped. Just when she thought they would get away free and clear.

They said their goodbyes to the Chief Inspector and walked out of the tiny office.

They waited at the desk outside his office for the officer to get off the phone. As they waited, Hester bent over to whisper to Lucy, "Maria! That might be Anna, the guide's, sister-in-law. Perhaps she is willing to help us."

Lucy's face lit up. "Yes!" she whispered back. "That would be wonderful. Especially, since we just missed getting sent to prison. I have to tell you, I was dang worried there for a minute."

"Me too." Hester sighed loudly. "I was imagining never again working in microbiology. Never seeing another great work of art. It was a grim thought."

And a quintessential Hester thought, Lucy mused.

Maria Lazzara's office was located one floor down, and to reach it Lucy and Hester had to pass through a large room packed with desks. The cacophony of ringing phones, people talking, printers spitting out reports, and the occasional shout across the room made Lucy feel instantly at home. A space much like this one had been her life for more years than she wished to remember.

Their chaperone led the way to an office at the far end of the room. A petite woman with short brown hair stood at a desk in front of the office, talking to the uniformed officer seated there. The woman wore a civilian business suit, and Lucy wondered if she had to purchase it in the children's section of the store, she was that tiny.

But upon closer inspection, Lucy noticed lines around her eyes and mouth and guessed her age to be in her late fifties.

A professional smile didn't make it to her eyes, as Maria waved Lucy and Hester into her office. She followed them in and sat down behind her desk. She indicated the two chairs facing her, and the women lowered themselves into them.

"Hello. I am *Vice Ispettore*, Deputy Inspector, Maria Lazzara. I heard from my sister-in-law, Anna, that you had an interest in a case." Lucy heard a hint of an English accent as if Lazzara had learned to speak English in England itself.

"Yes," Hester said. "I'm Hester Nilsson, and this is Lucy Tuppence. Lucy was on the scene when the body of the murder victim, Aurelia Carotti, was found in Burano."

Lazzara nodded once. "Yes. I know. I heard that you were in the building, and why. I'm working on that case."

Lucy smiled at the efficient state worker. She explained the reason for her interest in the murder case. When she mentioned having worked in law enforcement, Lazzara's gaze sharpened.

The deputy inspector sat silently when Lucy finished her explanation. She looked from one woman to the other, then down at a paper on her desk.

"I will let you know what I am allowed to, but you must promise me not to engage in foolish behavior like what you did in the victim's home, with the painting."

Lucy had assumed Lazzara would have known about the painting, so she wasn't surprised, but she was disappointed. It could make things more difficult for her.

"Thank you, I appreciate that," Lucy said. "*We* appreciate that," she quickly corrected with a wave at Hester. "May we ask about Aurelia's roommate, Laura Bacci. She was brought in last night for questioning, I believe."

Lazzara pressed her lips together as she stared at Lucy. Lucy waited her out. Finally, Lazzara said, "And here we have our first test. What can I say without losing my job? This is all. We do not believe she was involved in the robbery of the painting."

Hester perked up. "Oh, that's wonderful! Well, good. Good." She beamed.

Lucy reached over and patted Hester's leg. "I agree with my friend, that this news is good…but that doesn't get her off the hook for murder, does it?"

"No, it does not. In fact…and here, again, I walk a fine line…" Lazzara glared at Lucy. "It seems to have given her a motive for murder."

"What?" Lucy hadn't seen that coming.

"Laura Bacci knew about the painting. We have reason to believe she was blackmailing Aurelia."

Lucy's hand came down hard on the edge of Lazzara's desk. "I'm sorry. But if she was indeed blackmailing Aurelia, *why* would Laura kill the golden goose?"

"*That* I may not speculate on, not with you." She peered at Lucy for several long beats. "But if, as you say, you have law enforcement experience, you will be able to come up with an answer." The deputy inspector raised her brows and looked down her nose at Lucy. "I am sure."

Lucy wasn't sure she liked the woman's attitude. She sounded a bit snippy. Her back stiffened.

"Yes, you're right. I'm sure I will." Lucy sat silently for a few seconds before she asked, "If I may ask one last question. Has Aurelia's husband been questioned? Enzo Carotti?"

"With that law enforcement experience, I'm sure you know we would have questioned him first off."

"I assumed so. And…?"

"He is, shall we say, a person of interest."

"Did he have an alibi for the time of the murder?"

Lazzara rocked her head from one side to the other. "Perhaps it was not the most solid alibi we've ever seen."

"It sounds like Enzo could have motive, means, and opportunity, then."

Lazzara narrowed her eyes as she stared at Lucy. "As I said, he remains a person of interest."

Lucy stood, picked up her purse, and said, "Thank you for your time, Deputy Inspector Lazzara. I hope you will be able to chat with us again. Here's my card with my phone number and my email address." She placed the business card on the desk.

"Maybe I will be able to." Maria smiled at Lucy, and this time the smile reached her eyes. Lucy wondered what kind of game the woman was playing.

It wasn't until they were outside that Hester asked the question she'd been wanting to ask since leaving Maria Lazzara's office.

"Why? Why would someone kill a person they were blackmailing?" Hester asked Lucy, who was scanning the ugly area, trying to figure out how a person was supposed to return to the charming part of Venice.

Without taking her eyes from the task at hand, Lucy answered in a monotone, "The person being blackmailed refuses to pay. The blackmailer wants to scare them, so makes it look like they are going to kill the person, but during the scare, they accidentally kill the person."

Hester's eyes became large. "Ohhh…," she said with a sigh.

"I think we have to boat it back, but I'm not sure how to get to the dock from here. Follow me," Lucy directed Hester as she began a march around the building.

Lucy wasn't convinced that her scenario came anywhere near the truth. But it couldn't be dismissed.

Many a victim had been murdered when all the killer had intended was a good scare.

But Laura?

Lucy didn't buy it.

~ thirteen ~

LUCY, BEING THE ONLY ONE of their group who had not toured Teatro La Fenice, gawked at the interior of the concert hall. If for any reason, she hadn't yet felt like she was in Europe, this baroque, gilded extravaganza would have changed that quickly. The room had a magical quality, making Lucy feel like she'd left the reality of her own life and stepped into a fairy tale. Soft pale green walls were the only non-gold or non-red thing in the room. It could have been garish, with so much gold everywhere. But it wasn't. Lucy deemed it to be just the right amount.

The classical cacophony of instruments being tuned and warmed up emanated from the orchestra pit. Lucy felt the tiny hairs on her arms stand up, and gave herself a shake to remind herself that this was all real.

The slinky black, sleeveless dress she wore made her feel attractive and desirable. The undergarment that was holding everything in place felt considerably less sexy. And she was worried that one of her false lashes was only half adhered to her eyelid, as it seemed to flap in front of her eye each time she blinked.

They made their way down the sloped aisle to their seats, which Nicolo had made sure were some of the best in the house. Lucy spun slowly to take in the hall in all its grandeur before she scooted into their row. It was a breathtaking place.

They started across the row, to the center where they'd be sitting. Lucy's feet were screaming in the high-heeled sandals, and she looked forward to relaxing in the red velvet seat, which, like everything else, was elegant.

Lucy sat, and almost bolted straight back up. Clearly these seats had been constructed with skinny, hipless, ten-year-old boys in mind. How was a full-grown woman expected to sit comfortably in such a tiny seat?

Lucy turned to Carrie, who sat on her right. "Where are we supposed to put our hips?" she asked her, eliciting a giggle from Carrie.

"Yeah, good question. I was wondering the same thing." Carrie peered at Lucy's eye with the malfunctioning false eyelash. "Hey, Luce, did you know you have a lash that's about to fall off?"

Lucy's hand flew up to her eye. "What? I knew it was bugging me, but is it really about to fall off?"

"Maybe, but relax. I've got some eyelash glue in my purse. I'll take care of it for you at intermission."

Great, thought Lucy. *I'll miss seeing the first act of the opera what with the wiggly caterpillar on my eye.*

However, Lucy had no reason to worry about missing any of the opera due to a wiggly caterpillar because Carrie reached over and with one quick tug removed the offending lashes.

"I'll just put this is a safe spot in my evening bag until we do the repair," Carrie informed Lucy in such a way that Lucy knew better than to argue.

Moments later the orchestra pit fell silent, the lights in the hall dimmed, and the curtain rose.

For the next hour, Lucy sat with her mouth agape and her eyes wide open, nearly forgetting to breathe as she took in the spectacle.

The full ensemble impressed Lucy, but the man singing the lead was a glory all his own.

Nicolo Gavelli's performance was nothing less than magical. Lucy had become so immersed in the opera that when the curtain fell at the end of the first act and the lights came back on she had to take a moment to reorient herself, momentarily confused when she found herself surrounded by elegant people in an Italian opera house.

"Let's go take care of that lash," Carrie said, spoiling any last vestiges of operatic magic. She tugged on Lucy's hand, forcing her to stand. "Follow me. I know where the restrooms are."

After the reapplication process, Lucy and Carrie met Oscar and Hester in the lobby. As they approached Hester and her unrequited love, Lucy watched for any signs that Hester had taken this magical moment to reveal her hand. Oscar's body language shouted that she hadn't. He stood staring into the crowd, arms crossed, one toe tapping. Hester stood near Oscar, eyeing him, but saying nothing.

"Fabulous, just fabulous, isn't it," Lucy effused.

Oscar glared at her. "Really? Are you kidding? I'd rather get a root canal without anesthetic than to have to sit through any more of that wailing sound."

"Oh, now Oscar," Hester said, sounding more like a mother than a woman in love. "You must really give opera a chance. It is a wonderful experience if you just let yourself get immersed in it."

"Yeah. No," Oscar said, sounding churlish.

"Well, you're not getting out of this, Mr. Kapoor," Lucy said. "This performance is the best I've ever seen, and I've seen a lot of opera. You're going to sit there and *attempt* to understand why it is so magnificent."

"Yes, mommy," he snapped back.

"And, uh, Oscar," Carrie began, teasingly. "What happened to going with the flow and this being the best gig ever? Have you forgotten what you said to me back on Burano?"

Oscar's mouth became a fine line. "What I said didn't include incomprehensible opera."

Carrie laughed as she shook her head.

The lights flickered, and the group made their way, along with the crowd, back into the hall. Lucy, with eyelashes in place and aware that she looked good in her sexy dress, strode back in with a wiggle in her hips and her head held high, looking forward to Act Two with Nicolo.

An usher stood on the aisle next to their row, and as they started to scoot in, she said, "Excuse me, you are the Lucy party?"

All eyes shot to Lucy, while Oscar laughed. Ignoring her group she told the usher that yes, they were the Lucy party.

"Signor Gavelli asks to tell you to join him please for champagne after the performance in the Apollonian hall, if you please." The woman's English was so heavily accented that Lucy had to pause before answering to make sure she understood.

"Meet him? Yes, thank you." She smiled at the usher before making her way to her seat.

She wouldn't have thought it possible, but she was even more entranced by the performance, and by Nicolo, during the second act.

Lucy, Hester, and Carrie stood in a small circle on the elaborately inlaid wood floor in the Apollonian hall, sipping the refreshing Prosecco. The room, all white, gold, and mirrors, could have been a room in any European palace. And for the moment Lucy felt like a queen.

They had been waiting for nearly half an hour, and Lucy and Carrie were on their second glass of the sparkling wine. Hester still nursed her first. Oscar had been given a dispensation to return to the hotel.

Fifty or so guests filled the room, all of them awaiting the arrival of the star of the night's opera.

When he finally stepped into the hall, a hush fell over the assemblage for a just a few seconds before applause filled the room. One or two bravos were shouted. He wore a suit and dress shirt open at the neck. His thick hair was brushed back, but one lock had found its way to his forehead.

Nicolo smiled broadly, as he greeted the room. But Lucy could see him looking for someone.

When his eyes landed on Lucy, he stretched his arms out in front of him, palms upward as he hurried to her spot in the room.

Lucy beamed at him, feeling her face suddenly blaze.

"Ah, Lucy. Lucy. I am so very happy you made it to the performance tonight." Somehow knowing what was about to happen, Lucy handed her glass to Hester. Nicolo took both of her hands in his. Then turning to the others, he said, "And Lucy's friends, as well. I hope you all enjoyed the opera?"

He hadn't let Lucy's hands go, and she was in no rush for him to do so.

Finally finding her voice, Lucy said, "Nicolo, I truly have never been more moved by an opera in my life. That was simply glorious. And you, oh, well, you were *magnifico*!"

He smiled tenderly at Lucy, then dropped her hands and leaned to kiss first one cheek, then the other.

Hester and Carrie made sure to tell him that they, too, had loved the opera and especially his performance.

Nicolo made a self-deprecating shrug. "I simply use the gift the Almighty gave me. And it makes me happy to know you enjoyed it."

The three women chatted briefly with Nicolo, before he apologized for having to make a swift tour of the room to greet some of the other guests.

Lucy was on her third glass of Prosecco when he rejoined them. Hester and Carrie stayed for a polite minute or two before wandering off to another corner of the room, leaving Lucy and Nicolo alone.

"Truly, I have never been so moved by a performance. You were incredible. And the rest of the ensemble was pretty fantastic too."

He smiled a gentle smile. "You are too kind. I am very happy you enjoyed it. And I am hoping we might be able to have dinner later this week?" He cocked one brow.

Lucy fought her instinct to giggle. It seemed she'd gone back in time to high school.

"I would like that very much."

"Day after tomorrow? I have no performance that day."

Lucy grinned up at him. "Sounds perfect."

"Now tell me, Lucy, have you been enjoying your visit to our lovely city? What have you seen? Done?"

Lucy chose to lie by omission, knowing that he could be horrified if he heard what she'd really been up to. "*Oh, you know, the usual tourist things. Finding dead bodies. Searching flats I have no business being in. Finding famous missing paintings. Being called in by your police for some questioning at the Questura. Nothing too exciting.*"

After she shared the more appropriate version of events, he heartily approved of the itinerary to date.

Then his eyes ran up and down her body, appraisingly.

"Lucy, you look beautiful. And you've done something different with your hair, have you not? I like it."

Lucy stood a little straighter, and smiled warmly at Nicolo, enjoying his compliment.

He asked where she was staying, and told her he would

pick her up at eight on the evening of their date.

"I shall count the hours," he said, lifting her hand to his lips. Never in all her forty-plus years had a man kissed her hand. Of course, it took a trip to Italy for such a gesture to happen to her.

Lucy met Nicolo's eyes as he released her hand. She gave him a shy smile.

"I'm looking forward to it too. Very much." Lucy glanced around the room for her friends. "I know you need to do your rounds of the room, and I have an early start tomorrow, so I'll say goodnight for now. Thank you so much for a wonderful experience tonight."

"I am so happy you enjoyed it. *Buona notte,* Lucy."

"*Buona notte.*" She graced him with a radiant smile before heading toward the corner where Hester and Carrie huddled. As she made her way across the room, she hummed a strain from *La Dona e mobile.* She knew it would play in a loop in her mind all night. And she would welcome it.

~ fourteen ~

VERDI'S MASTERPIECES STILL PLAYED IN Lucy's mind the next morning as she put herself together for the day. She hummed one tune after another as she showered, put on her make-up sans eyelashes, and dressed in a sundress and cardigan she'd bought at the boutique. She grinned to herself at the thought that she was truly beginning the day with a song in her heart.

A loud rap on her door brought her back to the real world, but she didn't cease humming as she walked across the room to see who it was. Through the peephole, she saw Oscar.

"Good morning, Signor Kapoor," she sang out to him as she opened the door.

He scowled at her as he answered, "Uh, good morning? To you too?"

"Oh come on, Oscar! It's a gorgeous day. And we're in Venice. It really doesn't get much better than that."

"Agreed. Venice is amazing. But personally, I could do without of being awakened by all the church bells every

123

morning at six. Might have been quaint the first day, but not so much now. Why do they *all* have to ring them every morning? Couldn't they, like, take turns? One day St. Mark's gets a turn, another day some other church."

"Don't go turning into an old man at forty-five."

"Whatever. I came to show you the footage I had enhanced, if you're still interested."

For the first time, Lucy noticed the equipment Oscar carried.

"Yes, definitely. Come set up on the desk."

After Oscar had set up the monitor and found the selection he wanted to show Lucy, he pressed play.

Lucy peered at the screen, watching as the hooded figure hunched over the canal, stood up straight, and sauntered off in the opposite direction from where Oscar had been standing.

"Play it again, please."

Oscar reset it.

"Can you pause it right here?"

He hit the pause.

"Still can't really see a face, can you? But I can certainly tell we're looking at a man, not a woman. That's a big step forward."

"*If* this person really is the killer," Oscar pointed out much to Lucy's chagrin.

"Yeah, right," she grumbled. "Play it again."

When the footage ended, she stared at the blank screen.

"You're quite right that it may not be the killer. But consider this. Why would the person slowly stroll away from a dead body? Not raise an alarm of some sort? Not try to get help from someone nearby? That's odd, don't you think?"

Oscar nodded and shrugged simultaneously.

"And…we don't see what happened just before you started filming. Maybe we would have seen him put her in the canal."

"Why there? In such a crowded area?"

"Good question," Lucy said. "Maybe the current moved the body? Back in the area that he was walking back to it's very quiet, the end of the island. Just places for boats to dock and gas up. She might have gone in there, and the body floated down to where we saw it. If the tides were right."

"I suppose that's possible."

"Yeah, I think so too. You know, Oscar, I think this guy is either our killer or someone who knew something about the murder. I can't work out any other scenario that explains his actions here." Lucy tapped the black screen of the monitor.

Oscar's face lit up. "You said that's just an area to dock your boat? Maybe the killer came from Venice proper, docked his boat, killed Aurelia, and got away in his boat right after he killed her."

Lucy slapped Oscar's arm. "Yes! Yes, that makes perfect sense. Well done, Oscar."

"Except that the body had time to float. This far?" Oscar frowned.

"Let's worry about that later. I have another thought. I know you took this footage from an angle that didn't show that docking area. Any chance you have some that does show it?" Lucy raised her brows expectantly.

Oscar scrunched up his face. "I don't think so. The only other footage of that area was from the far side of the bridge you were on when you saw the commotion on the canal. The bridge would be in the way. I think." He knit his brows, thinking. "I can double check though."

"And could you put this footage on a thumb drive for me?"

"Yeah, no problem."

"That would be great. Thank you, Oscar. Now let's go meet the girls for breakfast and talk through our day."

Lucy waited while he quickly packed up the equipment and then they made their way to the terrace for breakfast.

The group had finished breakfast but were all enjoying coffee drinks—lattes, cappuccinos, Americanos—while they made their plans for the day.

"You know, Hester and I apologize that we had to scrap our plans yesterday," Lucy said, quite unnecessarily.

"Yeah," Carrie trilled. "When half of our group spends most of the morning at police headquarters being *questioned* it tends to put a wrench in our plans. At least two of us had a great walking tour of Venice. I'm sorry you missed it. It really was great."

"I'm sorry too," Lucy said to Carrie and Oscar. "I can promise you that Hester and I would have far preferred being with you touring this magnificent city than being questioned by the police and wondering just how dismal our prison cells would be."

Oscar and Lucy made polite chuckling sounds.

"But…" Lucy said in a voice that could be heard by several of the people at neighboring tables. "Today, we have no impediments. And despite the original agenda for filming, I would like to begin at Campo Santi Giovanni e Paolo."

Oscar looked skeptical. "Why?" He drew the word out.

"I believe that at this time of day the sun will be at a perfect angle to enhance the imagery."

"And how, exactly, do you know anything about where the sun will be? You've never been to this square." Oscar scowled at Lucy.

"Oh, but we have," Hester chimed in. "Lucy and I were there the other day."

Lucy rolled her eyes at Hester. *I'm going to need to talk to her about being circumspect, if she wants to help me on this case*, Lucy thought.

Oscar and Carrie peered at Lucy and Hester.

"So, Lucy," Carrie said in a singsong. "I'm guessing you need to *take care* of something while we're over there?"

"Perhaps. Maybe. We'll see how things are going." She lifted one shoulder in a noncommittal way.

"Okey dokey," Carrie said.

"I like the outfit," Lucy told Carrie, hoping to win a few points. Carrie was in a 'before the camera' outfit of slacks, cami, and denim jacket. A colorful scarf gave it all a bit of pop. Lucy knew she was trying to find the perfect balance between casual traveler and sophisticated professional. She'd done well.

"Oh, thanks. I think it works," Carrie said, running her

fingers over the scarf. "But contacts, or glasses?"

Carrie had a full collection of eyeglasses. Most were oversized cat-eye glasses, in a wide variety of colors.

"Do you have contacts in right now, or are you flying blind?"

"Blind. But really it isn't so bad. I'm thinking the aqua frames would be fun with this scarf."

Lucy knew that whatever she said would make no difference to Carrie, but she played along. "Absolutely. Go for it. The trendy, hip traveler look is perfect for our brand."

"Yeah. Think I will."

Lucy turned her attention to the full group. "Let's gather our stuff and meet in the lobby in fifteen."

What she didn't admit, or share, was that she was hoping to find and talk to Enzo Carotti while in his neighborhood. Lucy felt it was time for a proper interview with the grieving widower, whom the police still considered a person of interest.

By the time they were set up in the square the tourists were arriving, giving the background a good vibe, but it wasn't yet inundated with the travelers.

Carrie gave her first part a dry run, deemed it good, and went on to videotape it. When she and Oscar were setting up for the next shot in another area of the *campo* Lucy made her excuses to leave for a short errand.

The other three all gave her knowing looks. Hester asked if she needed any help on her errand.

She started to turn down the offer, but remembering her need for a translator, said, "Sure, if you want. Just in case I get lost and can't find my way back."

"When should we expect you back?" Oscar asked.

"We'll be back before you finish all your shots here. Remember to meet with the priest before you start the interior shots."

"Yes, ma'am."

"Keep him in line please, Carrie."

"Yeah, no problem. See you."

Lucy turned and strode toward the canal and its little, narrow walkway, with Hester following. This time Lucy knew exactly where she was going.

～ fifteen ～

EFORE OSCAR HAD ARRIVED AT her room that morning, Lucy had taken the time to examine the photos she'd snapped in Aurelia's flat. Those she took of the dresser top intrigued her the most.

Especially the picture of the young boy.

There had been no other pictures of anyone in her room. Only the one of the boy.

He obviously was of some importance in Aurelia's life. Lucy had decided that questions about the boy were the perfect excuse for a visit to her husband.

Hester hadn't asked any questions about Lucy's 'errand.' But when they stopped at the door that led to Enzo's flat, Hester said, "Are you sure you want to do this? That man looks dangerous. And we've heard he has a temper."

"I am sure. And I'm not worried about his temper."

"Okay," Hester said, sounding anything but okay.

They got in, climbed the stairs, and once in front of Enzo's door they both stood and stared at it for a good half-minute.

Lucy threw her shoulders back and knocked on the door. She could hear a television or radio. Enzo was home.

When the first knock went unanswered, she knocked again. This time she heard footsteps. Or more accurately, stomps.

The door swung open, and Enzo stood glaring at the two women, his mouth hanging open. Like the first time they encountered the man, he wore a tight T-shirt, but on this occasion there was a stain or two on the shirt. Lucy thought it looked like marinara sauce. Or perhaps, blood.

He growled a word that Lucy was unfamiliar with. She quickly looked to Hester.

Hester said something in Italian, her voice quavering more than usual.

Enzo answered with a bark, but waved them in.

Inside the small, dark apartment, the stench of fried fish assailed Lucy. Had the man breakfasted on fried fish, she wondered. She was more inclined to think the smell was a permanent fixture of the flat.

Lucy noticed Enzo eyeing Hester, who fidgeted as if uncomfortable.

"Tell him we had met Aurelia at the lace shop." Hester's raised brows made Lucy add, "He mustn't think we didn't know her at all."

Hester sighed before saying something to Enzo in Italian. He nodded, and Hester said to Lucy, "I added how shocked we were by her death."

"Good, good. Okay, so tell him we were wondering if they had any children, because if they did, we want to convey our condolences to them." Hester was about to translate this when Lucy said, "Oh! No, tell him that we wanted to convey our condolences to them by having a Mass said for their mother. Yeah. That won't sound so pushy. I mean, what Italian is going to oppose a Mass said for the soul of a loved one?"

"Right…" Hester gave Lucy a look that she assumed meant Hester thought she was losing her mind. But Hester passed along the sentiment in her perfect Italian.

Lucy watched Enzo as he listened to Hester, and saw his expression turn dark. She needed no Italian to understand the vicious *no* he growled.

Hester started to glance at Lucy, but Lucy stopped her. "No need. I got that. Ask, kind of casually, if she had any nephews or nieces who were special to her. That perhaps the Mass could be shared with them, instead."

"Really? I don't think I want to go there."

"It'll be okay," she reassured her friend, despite feeling none too sure herself.

"Fine," she whined.

Hester asked the question through gritted teeth.

This time Enzo didn't snap, but he did shake his head as he glared at Hester.

"Okay, let's cut our losses here. Tell him we're sorry to have disturbed him, that we are so sorry for his loss, and let's get outta here."

Even as Hester translated for her, Lucy began slowly moving in the direction of the door.

And as she did so, Enzo started moving in the direction of Hester.

Hester began stepping backward, away from the glowering man.

He grabbed her by the arm and wrenched her toward him. Hester squirmed to free herself without success.

Lucy didn't stop to think.

"Let go of her," she shouted in a tone that needed no translation.

She dashed over to Enzo, and kicked him behind one knee and, in quick succession, the other. He buckled enough for one arm to loosen on Hester. Lucy took the opportunity to grab his arm and pull it behind him. Hester, still held tightly by Enzo's free arm, lifted one knee and delivered a hard blow to Enzo's nether regions. He let her go, and Lucy grabbed the other arm and pulled it back as if she were going to cuff him.

She wished she had some handcuffs on her.

She made a mental note to add cuffs to her future packing list.

Hester ran for the door.

Enzo doubled over and wailed, while Lucy exerted pressure on her hold.

"Don't mess with us," she growled in his ear before releasing him and sprinting out the door.

Lucy found Hester waiting outside the door, and the two flew down the stairs.

Outside in the fresh air and sun, Lucy brushed her hands together as if removing Enzo from her skin.

She said, "Nice guy. Can't imagine why Aurelia left him."

Hester grimaced and shuddered.

"You going to be okay? You were awesome back there."

"Yeah," Hester said quietly. "But it wasn't a scenario I'd like to go through ever again."

"I can assure you. I have no plans of getting anywhere near Enzo again."

"Good. Because if you do, it's going to be without me."

"Deal." Then Lucy moaned, "I'm never going to get the smell of fried fish off of me."

"I know. That was quite malodorous."

Lucy stared at the eloquent Hester and giggled.

"Yep. That's one way of putting it."

"So, what was that all about in there?" Hester asked her. "I mean the part about the family members, not the part where he attacked me."

They started walking back the way they'd come, and even with only a dozen people wending their way through the exceptionally narrow *calle* conversation was impossible.

Over her shoulder, Lucy said, "I'll explain when we get back to the *campo*."

They hadn't been gone long enough for Carrie and Oscar to get a lot done, and they found them in the center of the *campo*, the monument directly behind Carrie, who was talking to the camera.

Lucy pulled Hester away and over to a bench where they sat.

"So, what that visit was all about," Lucy began. "When

we were in Aurelia's flat the day she was murdered, I noticed a photograph on her dresser. It was the only one there. I took a picture of it." She pulled out her phone and found the picture in question and handed it to Hester. "I figured this boy had to be someone important, right? I wanted to know if he might have been their son. Or someone else important. And as we learned, there was no son, and no special nephew or anything."

Hester slowly nodded once. "Oh…I see. So, who could it be?" She pushed her oversized sunglasses up on her head, using them as a hairband. The small gesture, done by hundreds of thousands of women every day, was done with a grace and finesse usually reserved for models who've been taught whatever trick it was that made the move look so sexy and elegant. The only thing that ruined it was the cellophane tape that held one earpiece to its corresponding lens.

"I don't know who it could be. But I was just wondering if there's some way that Oscar can age the picture. I mean, it's clearly a photo taken at least ten years ago, by the looks of the clothes he's wearing and just the amount of fading of the picture."

"You should ask him. Maybe he knows of some software that could do that. But then what? Say you get a picture of what this boy looks like today? What are you going to do with it?"

Lucy slumped forward and let out a loud breath. "I know, that's the problem that I can't solve. I can't exactly walk through all of Venice demanding to see all of the men between the ages of sixteen and twenty-five."

They both laughed at the idea, and in unison said, "Pervy!"

Hester interrupted their moment of levity. "And what about Enzo, himself? I'd say he has some issues."

"Aww, you say it so politely," Lucy said in a singsong. Then, in something closer to a growl, she added, "The man just attacked you, Hester. No need to be polite. I'd say he showed us today that he's capable of violence. Plenty capable."

Hester shivered.

Oscar ambled over to their bench, putting an end to their discussion.

"Hey, we still need to do the interior shots and Carrie's bit, but that's about it for here. I'm going to go in and check with the priest now. You wanna join me?"

Lucy was about to say yes but was struck by an idea. "If you think you and Carrie can handle it I'm fine with that. The only thing to keep in mind is that I have a boat and driver who's also a guide, booked for one o'clock at the dock by the Rialto Bridge. This side of it. We all should be there about twelve forty-five. You think you can make it over there and meet us?"

Lucy had arranged for a boat to take Carrie and Oscar up the Grand Canal for shots of the canal and everything around it, as well as a part with Carrie talking with the boat pilot about the points of interest along the canal. Lucy figured they would have to make at least three trips up and down the Grand Canal to get everything they needed.

"Yeah, no problem. We'll see you there." Then, screwing

up his face, he said, "God, you stink! Did you two fall into a vat of fish?"

"Something like that," Lucy growled. "Thanks for taking care things here. See you at the dock."

"Thank you, Oscar," Hester said in her most winsome voice.

"Yep," was all the response Hester got in return. Oscar hurried back to Carrie and all of his equipment. Together they gathered the cameras and lights, and then headed over to the main entrance of the church.

"Hester, don't let it get to you. He's just a distracted, blind man."

"I know," she agreed with a sigh.

"I have something to take your mind off of things. Come on. We're headed over to that Marco Polo neighborhood."

"You mean Aurelia's house." Hester sounded a bit peeved to Lucy's ear.

"No, not necessarily. More like the *calli* around there."

Hester stared at Lucy warily. "Is this for the travel video, or maybe looking for subjects for stills that could go in the magazine?" There was a hopeful note in Hester's voice.

"Maybe. Could be a reconnaissance trip. Or not."

Lucy put a hand on Hester's back and pointed her in the direction that she thought might be the right one.

But, she couldn't imagine how anyone could possibly know which way was which on the labyrinthine island. She could easily imagine some tourist from the 1990's still wandering through the many *calli*, going in circles, searching for his hotel. They say a person can't get lost in Venice because it's an island. But that doesn't mean someone couldn't perpetually meander from one *calle* to the next, from one canal to the next, from one *campo* to the next, never finding their destination.

As they took off from the *campo,* Lucy shook off a feeling of disorientation…or perhaps it was dread.

Only with the help of Hester's excellent sense of direction did Lucy make it to Marco Polo's neighborhood. While their pace had been brisk as they made their way across the island, once they arrived at Lucy's destination she began to stroll slowly.

"Whoa, Hester, I'm back here," she shouted to the tall blonde who was a good ten yards ahead of her, about to cross a canal.

Hester stopped and turned around. When Lucy reached her, Hester asked, "I thought you were in a rush to get to Aurelia's house."

"No…remember I said I wanted to walk through the neighborhood. We're in the neighborhood now, so it's time to slow down and take in all the sights."

Hester narrowed just one eye as she peered at her friend. "This is a sightseeing trip?"

"Of a kind, I suppose. I'm looking for someone. Someone who often seems to be hanging around here."

Lucy surveyed the area. The reflection of the canal played on the walls near it. A small boat made its way under the bridge. The sound of a TV could be heard coming from one of the flats directly above them.

"We know this person?"

"Nope. But I plan to get to know him."

"Really? I thought you were interested in Signor Gavelli, the opera singer."

"This isn't like that," Lucy said with a snarl. "This is someone of interest in Aurelia's case."

"Someone of interest," Hester parroted back at Lucy.

"Yes. As in suspicious. Or at least I find his movements of interest."

"You've seen him before?"

"Yes. I've seen him hanging around in the *calle* outside Aurelia's flat a couple of times. Like he's watching it."

Hester's brows inched up. "Okay, that is suspicious, isn't it."

"I believe so." Lucy described the young man and where she had seen him. Hester, with her near-photographic memory, immediately remembered him.

As they made their way along the *calle* and a few of the side *calli,* they both scanned the area. Lucy didn't expect the man would still be standing guard in front of Aurelia's home, but she thought there was a chance he might be somewhere nearby. He likely worked or lived in the area if he could so easily and frequently post himself in front of the flat.

They were walking past a small eatery with a large window in front when Lucy noticed the man sitting at the bar that faced the window. He was taking a bite of a panini when their eyes met.

Lucy put her hand out to stop Hester, without breaking eye contact with the man. He didn't look away or make any attempt to run. In fact, Lucy thought he looked like he was daring her to come in and confront him. She recognized the look. And she took him up on his implied offer.

"Follow me," Lucy directed Hester as she went into the eatery.

The stool next to the man was free, and Lucy sat down. Up close she could see he was much more of a teenager than a fully-grown man. His hair was curly and fell to just below his ears. Deep brown eyes had probably already gotten the attention of more than one girl. He was lean and wiry. In a T-shirt and jeans, he could have been a teen in just about any corner of the world.

Lucy and the teenager eyed one another warily before he looked up at Hester who stood like a bodyguard behind Lucy.

"Do you speak English?" Lucy asked him.

He shook his head, but said, "A little."

"Please tell him I've seen him hanging around the home of a friend of mine and was wondering why he was watching her home."

Hester did the translation. He stared at her, then at Lucy, but didn't say anything.

"Answer please," Lucy said sternly, ignoring the language barrier. She knew her tone and body language made her request plenty clear.

He shrugged.

"Tell him that the place he's been stalking is a crime scene and if he isn't careful the police will think he had something to do with the crime."

This time he said something in answer to Hester's comment.

"He said he knows."

Lucy leaned in close to the boy. "Oh, you do, do you? So why are you hanging out there?"

Hester waited a moment before translating.

His only answer was a shake of the head.

"Who are you? What is your name?"

Hester translated with precisely the same sharp tone Lucy had used.

He didn't say anything.

"I guess he doesn't want to talk, which obviously looks suspicious. He's guilty of something. Please tell him that if he changes his mind about talking, to meet me…" She stopped as she attempted to recall the next day's filming schedule. "To meet me at nine in the morning tomorrow. At, oh I don't know. How about on the steps outside the opera house, La Fenice."

After Hester relayed the message, the boy nodded once, then took a bite of his sandwich, signaling the end of their little tête-a-tête.

They left without further ado. Out on the *calle,* Lucy said, "That kid is hiding something. Or someone. He's definitely involved with Aurelia in some way. And I would put money on him knowing something. You don't just hang out around a murder victim's house."

"Maybe he's just drawn to the police action. Has a macabre interest in a murder case."

"If that were true he wouldn't have been so cagey with us. He would have told us that. And do you know why?"

"No, but I'm sure you're going to tell me."

"Because we clearly know something ourselves. We have been seen there. We would have information a stalker of murder investigations would want."

"True."

"That kid is hiding something, and we need to find out what it is."

They began their hike to the Rialto Bridge to meet Oscar and Carrie. Lucy's thoughts, however, weren't focused on the upcoming boat tour, but rather on a boy with a secret.

～ sixteen ～

KNOWING THAT SHE NEEDED TO be at the opera house a little before nine o'clock, Lucy had breakfasted before the rest of her gang. She was going over her notes for the day's filming when her phone rang.

As she picked it up, she noticed the time, eight twenty-eight. She'd need to get going soon.

"Hello, this is Lucy Tuppence," she said into the phone.

"Signora Tuppence, this is Deputy Inspector Lazzara." Lucy sat up, suddenly alert. "I'm calling in regards to the Aurelia Carotti case. I have some information if you are interested."

"Yes, I am. Indeed."

"I've just been told that the full examination of the painting has begun. They should have a preliminary report in a few days, though it won't be verified one way or another until more extensive tests are run."

"Well, thank you. That's good to know. Did they say that the preliminary report would be fairly conclusive?"

"*Sì,* they will have a good idea whether or not it is the stolen Canaletto after the preliminary investigations and tests. But it will not be fully conclusive."

"Deputy Inspector Lazzara, may I ask if you still believe Laura Bacci was blackmailing Aurelia?"

The line was silent. Lucy waited it out.

"Aurelia had made payments to Laura once a month. She has admitted to knowing about the painting's existence."

"She did? She knew about the painting?"

"Yes, this is what I said."

"Then did she say if she knew how the painting came to be in the apartment?"

"We did question her about that. She said Aurelia had told her it had always been in the family as far as Aurelia knew. Passed down from her grandmother."

"Then, if she was blackmailing Aurelia, then she knew that it was supposedly a stolen, missing masterpiece, right?"

Silence again.

Then, "This is more than I am able to comment on. And I must go now."

"Well...thank you. I appreciate knowing about the painting's exam. Please let me know if there's ever anything else you can share with me."

"Perhaps."

Maria Lazzara ended the call.

Lucy sat staring at the phone.

Despite Maria's assertions, Lucy felt something didn't add up. There was something there that didn't make sense.

Seeing the time, Lucy jumped up, leaving her notes

behind and not fully completed. She would have to text the others and tell them they would begin a little later.

Lucy was fairly certain she knew the way to the opera house. It wasn't far from the hotel. But she also knew that one wrong turn and she could end up somewhere on the other side of the island.

As she stood in front of the hotel, she looked right and then left.

Left.

She was sure that was how to begin the trip to La Fenice.

She took two steps in that direction, stopped, turned around, and stared in the opposite direction.

No, it was to the right, not the left. Lucy took off without any further second-guessing herself.

It was one minute past nine as she made the last turn that would take her to the opera house. Lucy hoped the boy wasn't overly punctual.

She walked the last few yards, across the small *campo*, to the opera house steps and saw the boy sitting in a beam of morning sunlight. He wore jeans and a leather jacket over a T-shirt and smoked a cigarette. His head was down as he stared at a step below the one he sat on.

Just as Lucy made it to the bottom step, the boy looked up. She smiled reassuringly at him.

And then panic struck her.

The boy had claimed he knew little English. What was she thinking, not bringing Hester?

Lucy, also wearing jeans and sneakers, lowered herself onto the step, sitting next to him.

"*Buongiorno,*" Lucy said. "I don't speak Italian. Do you think you might know enough English to speak with me?" She spoke uncomfortably slowly, carefully enunciating each word, each syllable.

He looked up at her. His eyes were only open to half-mast as if he'd just rolled out of bed. His brow was knitted.

"Some," he answered.

"Okay. I'll speak slowly." Patting her chest, she said, "I'm Lucy. Lucy. What is your name?"

He took a drag off his cigarette and blew out a cloud of blue-gray smoke before answering. "Giovanni Farone."

"Giovanni, did you know Aurelia Carotti?"

He nodded and took another hit off his cigarette.

"How did you know her?"

"No. I ask you. How did *you* know Aurelia?"

Lucy gave him a sad, closed-lip smile. "I didn't know her. I was at the canal when they found her body."

Giovanni tossed the cigarette on the step by his feet and ground it out with a sneaker. He ran a hand over his eyes and face.

"I'm sorry, Giovanni. Did that upset you?" Lucy was careful to keep an even, non-threatening tone in her voice.

For the first time since she'd arrived, Giovanni sat up straight. He looked Lucy directly in the eye.

"It is not…happy…is it?" he said.

Lucy shook her head. "No, it is not."

"How I know her?" His voice had gotten louder. "I barely

know her. Only a few months. Stranger."

Lucy maintained the eye contact. "Then why, Giovanni, were you watching her house after her murder? If you hardly knew her, that seems strange."

He nodded. "Strange. Yes."

His answers were beginning to infuriate Lucy. This was a game she had no desire to play.

"So…why do it? If it was a strange thing to do? You barely knew Aurelia."

"Yes, only knew her a little. For a two or three months."

Lucy clenched her fists at her sides and took a deep breath that she held for a count of five before she let it out.

"So, why?" she asked one more time.

"Because. She my *madre*."

∼ seventeen ∼

"**Y**OUR MOTHER?" LUCY SAID TOO loudly for the circumstances. She noticed one tourist's head jerk in her direction.

"*Sì.*"

"Then…but…you…" Lucy gathered herself before continuing. "But, Giovanni, you said you didn't know her."

His eyes locked onto Lucy's as he leaned toward her. "I never knew her. Not…uh…until I find her in *febbraio.*"

"Where?"

"No, no where. Uh, when. Month *febbraio.*"

Lucy face brightened. "Oh, February. You found her in February."

"*Sì*, yes."

"Giovanni, were you adopted?" Lucy worried the word would not be part of Giovanni's limited English vocabulary. "You grew up with a different family? Not with Aurelia?"

He nodded.

Lucy's heart became a hard mass in her chest. A tear began to form in one eye. Quickly followed by one in the opposite eye. She pressed a thumb and index finger to the inner corners of her eyes.

"How old are you, Giovanni?"

"*Diciotto.*"

Right, Lucy thought. She gave her head a shake.

He resorted to the preschooler method and showed ten fingers followed by eight.

"Eighteen!" Lucy cheered like a mother encouraging her three-year-old.

He smiled wryly and nodded.

"Had you been looking for Aurelia for very long?"

"No. Not until I turn eighty." Lucy giggled and made a note to herself to articulate better. Giovanni looked quizzically at her and appeared to be a little offended.

"No, no," Lucy said, waving it off. "I am not laughing at you for looking for her. Absolutely not. It's nothing." She waved it off with one hand. "So you didn't have to look for very long."

"No. Lucky."

Lucy looked at the boy more closely. She wasn't sure what Aurelia had looked like, but she was fairly certain this boy didn't resemble Enzo in any way. Giovanni's long, lean body alone shouted that Enzo had not shared his DNA with Giovanni.

Lucy brought her brows together and pressed her lips tight. She placed a hand on his upper arm before she asked, "And your father?"

He looked down at his feet. "No. I do not know."

"I'm sorry, Giovanni. But you did get to know your birth

mother. That must be some comfort to you. Made you feel good."

He turned his head to face Lucy, his expression suddenly dark. "Comfort? No. And yes. I wanted to know my father also."

"Oh. Of course." They sat staring at one another for several beats before Lucy asked, "Did you ask her who your father was?"

"*Si*," he growled. "She did not tell me."

"Oh. I'm sorry. But maybe she had a reason not to tell you."

Lucy could think of a half a dozen reasons a woman wouldn't want the son she gave up at birth not to know who his birth father was. None of them would make Giovanni happy.

"She say that."

Without breaking eye contact, Lucy nodded somberly.

"Giovanni, I am so sorry you lost your birth mother so soon after finding her."

His eyes darted around the area.

Lucy wondered if the police had found Giovanni and spoken with him. She would have liked to ask him but feared upsetting him at this point.

Instead, she asked, "Do you live here on Venice?" It sounded like a casual question, one asks a new acquaintance, but Lucy needed to know.

Giovanni shook his head. "No. Lido."

Lucy knew from her research that this was the long, narrow strip of land in the lagoon that acted as a suburb of Venice.

"With your family?" she asked with a smile.

"*Si*. And I love my *famiglia*. Good *madre e padre*."

"I know you do. And I am sure they are very proud of you. Love you very much."

Giovanni smiled. "*Si, si.*"

She took out a business card. "Look, if there is anything I can do to help you, please call this number. It is local." She pointed to the phone number.

He took the card and stuffed it in a pocket in his jacket.

"If I want to talk with you again, how can I find you?" she ventured, not expecting much.

"Most days I work at pizza. On Frezzeria." He pointed straight out from the steps. "Near the *piazza*."

"San Marco?"

He laughed for the first time. "Only *piazza* in Venice is San Marco."

Lucy made a small laughing sound. "Of course. I forgot. The rest are *campi*."

He touched his nose with an index finger. When Giovanni smiled, and it reached his beautiful eyes, he took on a handsomeness that wasn't yet apparent in his young face. But Lucy knew that one day soon he would be fighting off the girls.

"*Grazie*," Lucy said, holding out her hand to shake.

Giovanni took her hand and shook it.

He got up, reached back and offered Lucy a hand to help her up. A gentleman too. *Whoever had raised him had done a good job,* she thought.

They went their separate ways, Lucy to the hotel, while Giovanni headed in the direction of the *piazza*.

Aurelia had had a baby by an unknown father eighteen years ago. Lucy wondered who else might have known this.

No one had ever known about Lucy's baby.

At the age of nineteen, Lucy had found herself pregnant. The father wasn't a part of her life—it had been a college party one-time thing. After a week of agonizing over her options, she decided to have the baby and give it up for adoption. Through her parents she had known two couples who had waited for years before they'd been able to adopt, so having the baby felt like it could be a gift to someone desperately wanting a child.

But she lost the baby when she was five months along. Despite her plans to give up her son—it turned out it was a boy—she grieved for the loss in a way she would never have expected. Sometimes in the middle of the night, she would imagine the person or couple who would have adopted him and how they would never get to know or love their son.

Lucy knew what Aurelia had to have gone through, giving up her son. And she knew what a gift it must have been for her to meet him years later.

She also could imagine what it was like for Giovanni to meet his birth mother.

If she hadn't already committed herself to finding Aurelia's killer, she knew now that she wouldn't be leaving Venice until she could give Aurelia's son some form of closure.

～ eighteen ～

LUCY MET UP WITH HER group as they were finishing a leisurely breakfast. Today they were going to start their own walking tour of Venice and filming along the way. Because they had decided to begin with the less traveled areas, Lucy thought she could allow them a later start. By the looks on everyone's faces, they appreciated the break from the early mornings.

Carrie stirred sugar into her espresso as she met Lucy's eyes and smiled. "Lucy, good morning. We were just talking about that glassblowing island. Uh, Murano. When are we scheduled to visit? I'm hoping to buy some glass there."

"Not till the end of our visit. The day before we leave. And don't worry—you won't be the only one in our group buying some of that gorgeous glass."

Hester grinned and nodded her agreement with the Murano glass plan, before giving Lucy a serious look. "Did he show up?"

"He did." Lucy's tone was somber, at odds with the general joviality that the group had been enjoying when she sat down.

"Who?" Carrie asked, around a mouth full of pastry.

"There's been a young man whom we'd seen hanging around outside of Aurelia's flat. I thought he looked suspicious. Hester and I spoke with him yesterday, but he wouldn't tell us who he was."

Hester leaned in. "Did he tell you who he is?"

"Yep. He's Aurelia's son. She had him eighteen years ago and gave him up for adoption." Every eye at the table suddenly turned serious. "He only recently found her." Lucy swallowed hard and blinked rapidly. Her head bobbed several times.

When she thought she could continue, she said, "I'm going to find who killed his birth mother if it's the last thing I do." Her tone invited no argument.

Carrie looked down at her espresso. After pursing her lips, she finally said, "How do you know he didn't kill her? I mean, he seems like a good suspect. Angry because the woman who gave birth to him gave him away."

Lucy's mouth dropped open. She stared at Carrie. An uncomfortable silence fell over the table.

Eventually, Lucy broke the silence. "No. I'm sure that isn't the case. He's a nice kid. Was happy to meet Aurelia. Wanted to know who his birth father was, but Aurelia didn't tell him. I'm sure he didn't have anything to do with the murder."

"You sure you aren't being a little closed-minded because the kid appealed to your emotions?" Oscar asked. His tone made Lucy want to slap him. She felt her chest, neck, and face warm. Her first instinct was to snap back at him, denying his wrong-minded theory.

But then the cop mind took over for a moment.

Had she assumed too much because of her empathy for Giovanni and Aurelia?

With her eyes on Oscar, she answered, "You know, you could have a point there. And I will keep it in mind as I continue looking for the murderer. But, I still maintain that he had nothing to do with it."

Hester reached over and grabbed Lucy's hand and gave it a squeeze. "We know you'll maintain your usual professional perspective on it. I'm sure that was a sad story to hear."

Lucy nodded once. "It was." Her eyes were on the table.

"Well, at least you have your date with Nicolo to look forward to," Carrie said, an impish look on her face.

"Indeed, I do. And you know, I'm sure, that I will require a couple of hours to prepare, so we need to be back here no later than six." She smiled coyly. "He's picking me up at eight."

"You want me to help you with your eyelashes?" Carrie offered.

"I don't know about them. Maybe while we're out, we could find some that aren't so, oh, like giant caterpillars."

"Sure. We'll do it!" Carrie seemed almost more excited about Lucy's date than Lucy was. But, like Lucy, she was recently divorced, and Lucy knew that was a painful time in anyone's life. She suspected that Carrie was enjoying a vicarious thrill with the date.

"Thank you, Carrie. I know I'm in good hands with you."

Carrie smirked while she waggled her brows. "And maybe later tonight you'll be in someone else's *good hands*."

"Carrie!" Hester said in a rush of air. Lucy saw the peachy glow begin to blossom on her cheeks.

"Don't worry about it, Hester," Lucy said. "It's only silly girl talk."

Lucy knew that silly girl talk and Hester were not well acquainted. But if Lucy could somehow find a way to get Hester to proclaim her love to Oscar, perhaps she would find reasons to engage in a little girl talk with Carrie and herself.

So far, Lucy hadn't found any success on that front.

Seven forty-five. Lucy stood in front of the full-length mirror for the tenth time in the past twenty minutes. She felt like a girl preparing for prom, only more nervous, because she wasn't seventeen anymore but instead had nearly thirty more years on that seventeen-year-old.

Carrie had come through and had helped with hair and make-up, and Lucy was pleased with what she now saw in the mirror. She wore one of the dresses she purchased during her makeover day. It was a simple sleeveless A-line—the fabric a black background with large, colorful flowers dancing across it. She felt womanly and attractive. A new pair of sandals, with a more modest heel height than the other new pair, adorned her feet.

At precisely seven fifty-nine she started toward the lobby.

Nicolo stood in the center of the lobby, his hands casually in the pockets of his suit trousers. When Lucy approached him, he withdrew one hand from a pocket and took her hand.

He greeted her with a warm smile. "*Sei bella,* Lucy." He lifted the hand and gently kissed it. As he let go of her hand, he gazed into her eyes.

"I am so looking forward to our evening together," he said.

"As am I." She gave him a nervous smile. Dating elegant Italian gentlemen was a new experience for her. Even the concept seemed ludicrous to her at that moment.

But, fortunately for Lucy, elegant Italian gentlemen also know how to make a woman feel comfortable, at ease.

"I have a lovely place chosen for our dinner. I hope you like it. It is small. Intimate. Not flashy, so I hope you do not mind this."

"I like not flashy. Very much." She began to feel her jitters dissipate.

"It is not far from here. Near La Fenice. Shall we?"

He held out his arm for her to take. As she looped her arm through Nicolo's, she felt as if she'd been transported to a fantasy tale she had no business being in.

And she was determined to enjoy every minute of it.

Nicolo had told the truth. The restaurant was small and intimate. It was also elegant in an understated way. But most importantly, it was a place frequented by the local Venetians, not tourists.

Over wine and a flavorful *antipasto* of *Insalata Caprese*, they shared their life stories, or at least what each felt comfortable sharing. Lucy left out some of the less appealing details of her life and she sensed that Nicolo did too. Which was fine with her. This was a Venetian fairy tale after all.

Lucy did, however, tell him that she was the only child of hippies who had named her after listening to *Lucy in the Sky With Diamonds* while high. This got a loud, deep laugh from Nicolo. She also admitted that her youthful love for the indisputable facts of mathematics had most likely been a form of rebellion against her flaky parents.

"And how do you explain singing in a rock band?" he asked her, cocking one brow.

Lucy shook her head and shrugged. "All right. Maybe a few of the genes made their way through, after all." This time Nicolo's laugh got the attention of some of the other diners.

As they awaited their *primi* dishes—tagliatelle for Lucy— a violinist began to wander through the small room, playing a variety of classical pieces. Mostly by Italian composers. When he came to their table—playing something that sounded, to Lucy's ear, like Vivaldi—Nicolo ignored the musician and had eyes only for Lucy. With a gentle hint of a smile on his lips, he gazed at her. No man had looked at her like that in years.

The musician moved on only when their dishes were served.

"That was lovely," Lucy said, almost prayerfully.

"Ah, yes, that was from a Vivaldi concerto. Vito plays beautifully."

"You know the violinist?" Even as she asked the question, she knew she shouldn't be surprised that Nicolo would know many of the musicians in the city.

He laughed softly, musically. "Ah, yes. For many years."

They ate their way through their *primi* and *secondi* courses, chatting as if they had known one another for years. Lucy could almost imagine herself having been a lifelong Venetian. And she found it all too easy to get lost in Nicolo's smiling eyes. She tried to remind herself that this was vacation flirtation and nothing more, but she had little success convincing herself of this fact.

As they sat with espressos after their *secondi* courses, Nicolo said, "We can have our *dolce* here, or we can have something at Florian's after we dance." His eyes twinkled as he teased her with this unexpected choice.

"Dance?"

"Ah, yes, Lucy. In the piazza. It is a lovely night for dancing, do you not think so?" She found his sexy half-smile and one raised brow to be quite disarming.

Flustered, she said, "That sounds delightful." A small giggle punctuated her answer.

"I look forward to dancing with you, Lucy."

She gave him a warm smile in answer.

The check magically appeared, as if Nicolo had a secret code arranged with the wait staff. Lucy supposed it was possible—surely she was far from the first woman Nicolo had brought to the romantic restaurant.

But on this night she cared little about Nicolo's previous conquests.

She was allowing herself to live the *dolce vita* for once in her life.

Even before they strolled into the square, Lucy heard the strains of music.

As they stepped through the arches of the arcade and into the *piazza,* she felt a sense of enchantment wash over her. What she saw before her was unlike anything she had ever experienced in her life.

Lit only by the rows of lights on the buildings surrounding the square and the stars above, couples danced, small groups wandered, lovers kissed, children ran and giggled. All accompanied by the live music filling the ancient *piazza.* And watched over by the magnificent basilica, which, in the night, looked like something from a magical fable.

Unlike during the day, the square wasn't crowded with tourists, most of whom had retired to their cruise ships for the night. Venice at night is a Venice returned to its citizens. And some of those citizens were enjoying an evening in their *piazza.*

Nicolo, one hand on Lucy's waist, guided her to a spot not far from the bandstand.

Without ever taking his eyes from hers he pulled her to himself, an arm around her waist and his other hand holding her free hand. He lowered his head to her ear.

"Vivaldi again. I think he must be serenading us tonight."

Indeed, Lucy thought. She didn't recognize the music as Vivaldi's but who was she to question a Venetian opera singer? The truth was she knew little of his work beyond the

Four Seasons. Besides, all of her senses were focused on how she felt in Nicolo's arms.

A Strauss waltz followed the Vivaldi and Lucy soon felt out of breath as Nicolo spun her about the square with great vigor. She was thankful when a slow piece of music from a movie soundtrack, which she couldn't identify, was played. Nicolo pulled her close, and she rested her head on his chest as they moved together to the music.

Lucy did, however, recognize the first notes of the next piece of music. It had been a guilty pleasure she'd long loved. The tango from *Evita*. Now, hearing those first notes, they struck terror to her heart.

A tango.

Nicolo stood tall, his hands ready to lead Lucy. She prayed he wasn't planning on her performing feats of magic with her body, but instead could guide her through a modified version of the intense dance.

It was the last coherent thought Lucy had for the next ten minutes.

She found herself in some place, some dimension, she'd never known existed. She needn't have worried about her lack of tango-ability. Nicolo led her through it in such a way that Lucy might have been dancing tangoes all her life.

The last note of the tango still hung in the air when Nicolo cupped Lucy's face in his hands. With the stars making a canopy above them Nicolo gently kissed Lucy. It had been years since she'd last been kissed like that and she was pleased she hadn't forgotten how.

~ nineteen ~

L UCY WOKE UP HUMMING.

She wasn't sure what the tune was but suspected it might have been Vivaldi.

She grinned and wrapped her arms around herself.

If she felt a little more energetic, she might have jumped out of bed and danced about the room while singing that she could have danced all night.

Sitting in bed, grinning to herself, she recognized the emotion she was feeling. It was one she hadn't felt in years.

Giddiness.

Giddy like a schoolgirl.

Lucy and Hester had given everyone the day off. There was no rush for her to get to breakfast. But an espresso was sounding awfully good, so she forced herself out of bed and stumbled across the room to the bathroom where she started the water in the shower.

While she was waiting for the water to get hot, she received a text. From Nicolo. Lucy read it with a wide smile on her lips and texted him back. At the end, she added a heart emoji.

The water was hot—steam filled the small bathroom. She put aside the phone. Perhaps she would treat herself to just one or two songs in the shower, she mused.

Maybe a little Vivaldi opera. Or something from *Evita*.

It was nine-thirty when Lucy moseyed out onto the breakfast terrace. Most of the tourists had eaten and were out exploring the city, so few tables were occupied. Lucy's eyes found Hester sitting at one of the prime tables along the balustrade, where there was an attractive view of the *calle* and neighborhood.

"I'm surprised to find you here so late in the morning," Lucy said as she joined Hester. She had never known Hester to be anything other than an early riser. And one who always was replete with more energy than any one person needs for the early morning hours.

"Oh, good morning! Yes, I stayed in bed and read for an hour. I know what you're thinking. How decadent." She grinned mischievously. "But I loved it!"

"I'm so proud of you, Hester." Lucy gave her friend a brilliant smile. And Lucy wasn't teasing—she was genuinely impressed that Hester had found it in herself to relax.

"So…how was your evening?"

Lucy rested her elbows on the table, laced her fingers together, and settled her chin on the bridge her fingers formed. With a deep sigh as she gazed into space, she answered, "Magnificent. Marvelous. Amazing. I mean, exactly what you'd think an evening in the most romantic city in the world spent with a handsome opera singer would be like." She punctuated this with a laugh that sounded more like a sound a squirrel might make.

"That's wonderful!"

"It was. And you know what? I am making it my mission that before we leave this little slice of paradise, you and Oscar will dance under the stars in Piazza San Marco."

Hester rearranged her silverware, then adjusted the placement of the salt and pepper shakers. "Oh, I don't know about that."

"Then, just think of it as something for our research. To be able to report on the opportunity. One few tourists take advantage of."

Hester ventured a glance at Lucy. "Oh, I don't know."

"This is something I'm going to make sure you, Carrie, and Oscar get to experience. It is truly like heaven."

"Maybe you and I could dance," Hester suggested, her brows pulled together.

"Hester Nilsson. I have some news for you. You're gorgeous. Men notice you everywhere you go. If you want to dance in San Marco Square, you could have your choice of any man there." Lucy turned up one side of her mouth in a lopsided smile. "And… maybe you should dance with some stranger. Make Oscar a little jealous. You know?"

"Oh, I don't know."

"You're starting to sound like a broken record. Stop saying that. Time to be a woman of action."

"Well, we will see."

Lucy gave her a naughty smile.

"Uh, so, what shall we do today?" Hester asked, in a clear attempt to change the subject.

"I thought we could take a leisurely stroll, maybe to some area we haven't been to yet. Stop and have some gelato. Maybe a coffee. Simply take in the atmosphere without worrying about travel business."

"Or the murder case?" Hester gave Lucy a look like a mom would give a child when the kid was supposed to stay away from the TV or video game.

"Yep. No murder case today either." It was a lie. She had hoped to spend some time in the afternoon talking to Lorenzo about Aurelia and finding out if he knew anything about the painting.

"Well, if you promise that, I think a stroll sounds lovely."

"What sounds lovely?" a colorfully dressed Carrie asked as she pulled out a chair. She wore a multi-colored striped skirt that fell to her knee, a bright yellow shell with a matching short-sleeved cardigan, and red-framed glasses. Lucy felt dull in comparison, in her denim capris and blousy cream shirt. But she did feel more comfortable than she had in days.

"Stroll. Gelato. Coffee. Relaxing," Lucy said.

"Yeah, that sounds great to me." Then with a naughty grin, she asked, "And how was the date with the gorgeous opera singer?"

Lucy's sigh was almost musical. And she launched into another poetic retelling of her magical evening.

When she'd finished her tale, Carrie gave her a sidelong glare and asked, "Yeah, yeah, yeah…but what about *after* the dancing and romantic moments under the stars?"

Lucy stuck her nose in the air. "I have no idea what you're talking about."

"Oh, yeah, right. Lucy Tuppence, you owe it to Hester and me and our complete lack of romance to dish on what happened. Later on…"

Lucy gave Carrie a lopsided grin. "Well, here's the problem with that. If I say that nothing happened, you'll be angry with me for not living the full *la dolce vita* in proxy for you. And if I admit that something did happen, you'll think I'm a fast moving hussy." She made a clicking sound with her tongue as she narrowed one eye. "So, you see, it's a lose-lose proposition for me."

Carrie leaned toward Lucy, her mouth hanging open, her eyes glaring. "You. Are. Evil."

Lucy chuckled. "That is my only goal in life, Carrie."

When the three women left Oscar behind at the hotel, it was with strict instructions that whatever else he did that day, he was to meet them in Piazza San Marco at ten o'clock that evening. He had told them that he had plans that involved boats and climbing to high places, but that he would be willing to meet them that evening.

The women met outside the hotel. Carrie wore her outfit of many colors now topped off with a straw hat. Lucy was in her dull, but comfortable denim. And Hester had dressed in something that made her look like a Vestal Virgin. Filmy, flowing, yards of white fabric caressed her body in a tunic and wide-legged pants.

"You doing a modeling shoot today, or something?" Lucy teased her. "You look way too good to be hanging out with the likes of us."

"You get that here?" Carrie asked Hester.

"Yes. It is supremely comfortable." Her eyes twinkled.

Lucy examined the neckline and cuffs for any signs of forgotten price tags. Somehow, they all seemed to have been removed. A first. But all that white fabric. She'd have to make sure to steer her toward the vanilla or coconut gelato. No strawberry or chocolate in Hester's future.

Without a plan, they started ambling toward the Rialto Bridge. When they got there, they discussed the pros and cons of their choices, then went ahead and crossed it, turning left on the other side. They made their way through the throngs of people that always swarmed the Rialto and its nearby areas.

Hester, being significantly taller than either Carrie or Lucy, was their guide through the crowds, as she could see what was ahead.

They had only walked a hundred yards from the bridge when Hester tapped Lucy on the arm.

"Lucy. I think I see Enzo up ahead."

Lucy walked on her tiptoes, trying to see around the people ahead of her.

"Where?"

"Wait a second, and you'll see them."

"Them?"

"Yes. He's with a woman."

"Anyone we know?"

"No. I don't think so. She looks like she could be a prostitute." She said it like it was a simple statement of fact, not a moral comment on the woman's appearance.

"Yeah, we don't know any prostitutes," Carrie shot back at Hester. "At least, not here in Venice."

Carrie and Lucy exchanged a look as they shared a silent laugh.

Another ten yards along the canal and the crowd parted. Lucy caught a glimpse of the couple, not far ahead. Enzo had an arm around the woman's waist. She was whispering something in his ear.

"Carrie, give Hester your hat. Hester, pull your hair up and stuff it in the hat. Then sidle up to the couple and see if you can hear them."

"What? Why?" Hester asked, even as she took the hat Carrie handed her.

"I'd like to know who she is. See if you can at least catch a name."

"He might recognize me."

"Not in that get-up he won't. And the hat will hide your hair pretty well. Make sure you keep those sunglasses on."

"Can Carrie come with me? He doesn't know her."

"Good idea, yes."

Lucy expected a groan or other complaint from Carrie, but her face brightened at the prospect of a little stalking assignment.

Lucy watched from a safe distance as Hester and Carrie moved closer to the strolling couple. She had to admit Hester had a point about the woman's appearance. She did have a certain prostitute-like look about her. The woman wore a red skirt that was about a size too small for her generous hips, and a lacy, low-cut top that was a good two sizes too small. When she turned toward Enzo Lucy could see the woman's large breasts look as if they would escape the clingy top at any moment. Her hair was dyed an unnatural shade of blond—it was more of a yellow. She teetered on stiletto heels.

And she giggled at everything Enzo said.

Hester walked along, on one side of the couple, and Carrie took up the other side. They moved naturally with the tourists walking along the Grand Canal.

Then Enzo and the woman stopped suddenly. Hester and Carrie continued walking. Lucy was impressed with the professionalism they brought to their stalking.

Lucy slowed her pace as she saw Enzo take the woman in his arms and kiss her right there in the middle of the *fondamenta*. This wasn't a gentle parting kiss. This was a long, passionate kiss. She wanted to look away, but she couldn't.

It was like watching a train wreck.

If she didn't stop walking she would run right into them, so she turned and pretended to watch the boats on the canal. But she kept one eye on Enzo and his lover.

They finally parted, and Enzo turned to walk back the way he'd come. Lucy made sure she kept her back to him.

When he'd passed, she looked back in the direction of where they had been kissing. She didn't see the woman now, but she did see Hester, who was turning into a side *calle*,

Carrie at her side. It looked like they still had the woman in their sights.

Lucy hurried to catch up with them.

As she moved in next to Carrie, she said, "You two follow my lead. Hester, I might need you to do the talking."

Lucy scanned the area in front of her until she found the woman. She'd stopped to buy a gelato.

Perfect, Lucy thought.

"Looks like we have an excuse to get those gelatos now," Lucy told them with a grin.

The three women stepped up to the gelato counter, making sure they were directly next to the mystery woman. Lucy surveyed the gelato offerings. Each flavor was heaped high in its tray, looking sinfully inviting. The rainbow of colors made her mouth water.

Lucy whispered to Carrie, "Please order me a scoop of passion fruit in a cup. And watch what Hester orders. All that white." She grimaced.

"Sure."

Then Lucy turned to the woman. Up close she looked to be pushing fifty, but she thought it might have been the effect of the heavy make-up.

"Ahhh!" Lucy, with a massive smile on her face, squealed at the woman. "*Buongiorno*! I can't believe I ran into you."

The woman first looked dazed, but her expression quickly turned dark. She muttered something in Italian. Or Venetian.

Lucy asked Hester to translate. "Tell her I'm sorry, I thought she was the woman who was going to be on our TV show."

Hester frowned. "What?"

"Please just say it. I'll explain later."

Hester translated, but without her usual vigor.

The woman's expression lightened. She said something in answer to Hester's comment.

"She says it's okay and asks what kind of TV show are we making. Which is something I wouldn't mind knowing, too."

"A show about travel in Venice. Of course." She scowled at her friend.

Hester answered the woman.

Lucy made a face that looked like she'd just found out she'd won the lottery and clapped her hands together.

To the woman who couldn't understand a word she said, Lucy enthusiastically suggested, "Perhaps you would like to be on the show too?" The woman stared at the loud American, a look of confusion on her face. But Lucy ignored it. "We are looking for people who live right here in Venice to talk about what it is like to live with so many tourists always in their city. The good, the bad, and the ugly."

Lucy, smiling a closed-lip smile, turned to Hester, and waved at the woman.

Hester again translated. Lucy watched as the woman's eyes began to sparkle.

"Oh, *si, si, si.*" The rest of her exclamations Lucy didn't understand, but it didn't matter. She got the reaction she was hoping for.

"Ask her if she can meet us for filming at two o'clock this afternoon at Campo San Stefano. By the monument."

After Hester relayed the information, the woman nodded vigorously.

"Wonderful!" Lucy told her. "And what is your name?"

With a wide grin, she answered without translation. "Fausta Patela," she sang. Lucy realized '*what is your name*' was probably a sentence most Italian schoolchildren learned.

"Fausta, I am Lucy." She then introduced Hester and Carrie. "Thank you for agreeing to help us with our TV show." The last bit Hester quickly translated.

They finished up with goodbyes and thank yous.

After Fausta left with her double-scoop of something with chocolate and scads of caramel, the three friends-cum-sleuths, picked up their cups of heavenly treats and continued their stroll along the canal.

"So, what exactly do you have planned?" Carrie asked.

Lucy finished savoring a bit of tart passion fruit gelato before answering. "We're going to see if Oscar would mind meeting us and filming for us. We're going to interview Fausta, but I'm going to make sure I steer the conversation in a direction that will give me some much-needed information. I hope."

"But Oscar's going to be on boats and climbing… things," Hester unnecessarily reminded Lucy.

"Maybe he'll be able to make a little time for our project. If things go the way I'm thinking, he won't need to be there very long at all."

"What if he can't?" Carrie asked.

"Then we get his camera and pretend that we know what we're doing. All we have to do is make it *look like* we're filming for a TV show. She won't know the difference."

Carrie grinned and raised her brows. "I'm starting to like this detective stuff."

Hester shot her a cautionary look. Lucy knew that all of this subterfuge was outside of Hester's comfort zone.

But then again, so was dancing in the square with Oscar, but she was going to make sure she did dance. Under the stars. With the man she'd loved for most of her life. It was something she owed her best friend.

There was nothing wrong with straying outside of one's comfort zone now and then.

~ twenty ~

LUCY, HESTER, AND CARRIE EACH stood on different sides of the monument in the center of Campo San Stefano, watching for Fausta. It was just before two o'clock. Lucy had managed to get a begrudging agreement from Oscar to arrive at the *campo* at two forty-five.

A dozen or so people sat on the steps of the monument, and no more than twenty-five or thirty others strolled around the small square. The afternoon sun was becoming uncomfortably hot, and Lucy began to wish she'd changed into a skirt. Carrie had removed her cardigan. And Hester looked as cool and calm as could be in her Vestal Virgin ensemble.

Lucy hated her for it.

As she waited for Fausta to appear, Lucy gazed at the leaning campanile, or church bell tower, that loomed over the square. Tall and slender, it was built of dark brick. The angle of its lean seemed precarious, to her eye. She'd noticed a leaning campanile on Burano as well. Evidently, Pisa didn't have the only leaning tower in Italy.

At two minutes before the hour, Carrie sounded the alarm—she'd spotted Fausta.

They gathered together, smiling and waving at her.

Fausta had changed her clothes. Now she wore a layered black dress. The underlayer was a form-fitting, short sheath, over which a see-through layer of black, filmy fabric fell to just above her knees. Like her morning clothing, the dress was at least one size too small. On her feet, she wore stiletto heeled, bright pink, ankle boots.

She sashayed her way across the square to join them. As Fausta got closer, Lucy could see her picking at her dress— pulling, smoothing, adjusting. Closer up she noticed a fine sheen of perspiration on her face. Lucy recognized nerves when she saw them.

Lucy and Hester had already run through what Hester was to say in greeting.

Lucy listened as Hester's melodic Italian informed Fausta that their cameraman was running a little behind schedule, and perhaps she would like to sit and enjoy a glass of wine at the cafe on the square.

Fausta wasted no time taking them up on their offer.

Seated at a table outdoors on the square with a bottle of Italian red wine and three glasses, the women chatted through their interpreter, who was sticking to sparkling water as usual.

They had agreed beforehand that Lucy would talk, pause and wait for a translation, and then continue on, like a journalist's interview with a foreign dignitary.

Lucy was careful to make their chat sound like the universal female small talk. Is she married? Yes. The answer didn't surprise Lucy. Any children? One, a girl of fifteen. Work outside the home? Fausta had just lost a job, she told them.

When Fausta poured herself a second glass, Lucy dug a little deeper.

"I have a question," Lucy said, then waited for Hester's translation. "This will sound strange, but we're from the States, and you know how people there can be, oh, prudes." Lucy personally didn't believe this, but it worked well for her narrative.

Fausta giggled and nodded.

Lucy feigned coyness. "You being Italian, have you ever, you know, taken a lover?" Lucy quickly covered her mouth as if the very question was far too embarrassing for her.

Fausta laughed loudly.

Lucy waited impatiently for Hester's translation. By the shocked look on Hester's face, Lucy knew the answer was going to be exactly what she was hoping for.

"Yes, of course. In fact, her, uh, current lover, is her sister-in-law's husband."

Lucy almost shouted, "What?" but caught herself when her mouth was half-open.

That wasn't exactly what she was anticipating.

"She's married to her lover's wife's brother." Hester not only had to translate from the Italian but had to be careful not to use any names. Lucy appreciated her talent.

"Oh, my. Only in Italy. Wow." Lucy said, smiling at Fausta but speaking to Hester and Carrie.

Lucy glanced at Carrie and saw her stifling a laugh.

Still smiling at Fausta, Lucy continued. "So she knows a lot about the victim's family. Since she is a member of the same family. You can say whatever the heck you want to her for a second, Hester. Cover up for my little commentary while I think."

Lucy gave herself a shake and took a large gulp of wine.

"How interesting that you and your lover are members of the same family. It must be hard to hide your affair."

If Hester had looked a bit pale after the earlier answer, this answer turned her the same color as her Vestal Virgin get up.

"They don't hide it because everyone knows," Hester said quietly, through gritted teeth.

"Well, isn't that convenient," Carrie said before biting her lip to fight off another laugh.

"Just a second," Lucy said. "There's got to be a way to use this. I need a moment. Talk about the weather or something." Lucy's words were rushed and barely intelligible. "No, ask her about what life in Venice is like when the citizens have to share their space with hordes of visitors."

While Hester and Fausta discussed the pros and cons of Venetian life, Lucy came up with a plan. Whether it would work or not, she couldn't be sure. But it wouldn't hurt to try.

First, she texted Oscar to ask him to give them an extra fifteen minutes.

Then she turned her most dazzling smile on Fausta.

"Please tell her I'm curious about how she gets along with her sister-in-law."

"But she's, you know," Hester said. Then behind a hand, she whispered, "Dead."

"Exactly." She continued to beam a smile Fausta's way.

Lucy listened and watched Fausta's face and body language as she and Hester talked. After Fausta spoke Hester said something back before she translated for Lucy.

"Her sister-in-law just died recently."

"And you gave her your condolences?"

"Yes."

Exchanging the smile for a more empathetic, mournful look, Lucy said, "Tell her I'm so sorry. Was it cancer? Her heart?"

Hester stared at Lucy for a few seconds before posing the question to Fausta.

"No. It is very sad. She was murdered."

Lucy opened her mouth wide in feigned shock and put her hands on her cheeks. "No. How tragic. Oh, wait, was her name Aurelia Carotti? I heard about that murder. Say it exactly like that, please."

"Yes, it was Aurelia. She can't say she is sad she is gone, but her husband, Aurelia's brother, is most heartbroken."

Without taking her eyes off of Fausta, who was helping herself to the last of the wine, Lucy said, "You know of course, that what we have here is a perfect suspect. As is her lover."

Lucy gave Fausta a sad smile, and then turned her eyes to Hester and Carrie. They each gave one another meaningful looks. Looks that said, 'We've got something big here and need to tread carefully.'

Not ten seconds after their telepathic conversation, Oscar, lugging his video equipment, stepped up to the table.

"Please excuse me to Fausta for just a moment," Lucy said.

She got up and led Oscar further into the square.

"Look, we have a chatty, tipsy murder suspect here." She filled Oscar in on everything Fausta had told them.

After a dramatic eye roll, he asked what he could do to help.

"We just need some time. I doubt we'll even get to the point of needing to actually film anything, so don't make much of an effort to set up. Just do enough to make it look legit."

"Sure thing. Where?"

"Oh, I don't know. Maybe over there to the left of the monument. Thanks, Oscar."

Lucy returned to the table.

To Fausta, whose nose and cheeks had become quite flushed with the wine, she said, "It will take him a little while to set up. We certainly appreciate you doing this for us."

"She says she's excited to be on American TV."

"Say, so, while we're waiting, I was wondering if the police have found Aurelia's murderer?"

Fausta's reply needed no translation.

She gave one sharp laugh.

Then, shaking her head she spoke, her words sounding agitated.

"Oh my," Hester said to Lucy as an aside, her eyes huge. "She said, the police are no good at anything. She knows this because she knows things about Aurelia's family that the police have never discovered."

"Oh, my God," Lucy said under her breath.

Carrie whispered, "You gonna to ask anything about that?"

"You better believe I am."

Returning to her concerned, empathetic look, Lucy said to Fausta, "What have the police never discovered?"

Fausta looked to the left, and then to the right, and finally behind her. Then she leaned far into the table, and in a whisper said, "Nazis. Her family was mixed up with Nazis." She nodded, gravely.

~ twenty one ~

"HOW DO YOU MEAN, MIXED up with the Nazis?" Lucy asked, her voice only loud enough for Hester to hear.

After Hester posed the question, Fausta played with the tablecloth before answering.

Back and forth, Hester continued translating the conversation.

"Aurelia's grandmother was involved with a Nazi during the war. Or maybe more than one." Fausta raised her brows to emphasize her assertion.

"When you say, involved with, do you mean she was having an affair with a Nazi?"

Fausta nodded.

"She did favors for them during the war. Her husband, that would be Aurelia's and my husband's grandfather, was big in Mussolini's army. I think that's how she met the Nazis."

Lucy felt her heart and lungs constrict, and fought to take a breath. She was so close now to the mystery of the painting.

And probably the answer to Aurelia's murder.

"What did they do for her in return for her favors?"

Fausta shrugged. "No one has ever really known, though there are all kinds of rumors." Lucy waited her out, knowing she wouldn't be able to leave it there. "Like gifts of jewels stolen during the war. Or of silver and gold. Or of works of art."

"Did Aurelia's family seem well-off? Like they had more money than other families?"

Fausta shook her head.

No, of course they weren't, Lucy thought. The priceless painting never left the closet.

"Fausta, do you think someone might have known this and killed Aurelia because of it?"

"Maybe."

"But who would have known?" Besides you, Lucy thought.

"My husband. Her husband. Her boyfriend, Lorenzo. Maybe the woman she worked for."

An idea struck Lucy. "How long did you know Aurelia?"

"Oh, since we were children."

"Was Aurelia's first and only job, lace-making?" Lucy knew she was crossing a line and was no longer acting like a supposed TV producer. But she sensed that Fausta was enjoying the attention, and with the wine in her system had to be feeling rather relaxed. So Lucy chose to press it as far as she dared.

Fausta shook her head. "No, no. First, she worked in an office. She really hated it. Left the job to go to Padua and apprentice with an old Burano lace-maker who had retired there. When she got back, she only ever made lace. And she was very good at it." For the first time since they had started talking about Aurelia, Fausta sounded melancholy.

"Can you remember about when it was that Aurelia went to Padua for her apprenticeship?" Lucy bit her lip while she waited for Hester to translate. She watched as Fausta considered the question, squinting her eyes as she stared at a spot in space and made tapping motions in the air, like she was doing a math problem.

"I think it was about twenty years ago, though it could be less. Maybe seventeen or eighteen years."

Lucy's heart raced, and she took a deep breath to calm herself.

"You said she worked in an office. Do you remember what office? Or what kind of business it was?"

Fausta pursed her lips and shook her head. "No, all I remember is that Aurelia hated working there."

"Was it the job she hated? Or the people? You know, the atmosphere?"

"I think it was the people. I remember hearing Aurelia complain about a few of them."

"Would Enzo know where she worked?"

"No, she didn't know Enzo back then."

Before she continued translating Fausta's answer, Hester's brows inched up. She added, "She's asking when we will film her, and she thinks these questions are getting odd."

"Okay. Of course. Tell her I'm going to go ask our cameraman."

Lucy got up and walked over to where Oscar was playing with his camera. "Pretend you're telling me that there's a problem with the camera." She knew Fausta's eyes were on her.

"Why? What's going on?"

She figured those were enough words for the play-acting and scowled at Oscar, then pointed at a dial on the camera. With the scowl, she said, "I have all the information I can get from her, so we're going to cut and run. Look upset."

"No problem there," he spat, shaking his head. "You got me while I was climbing the campanile at San Marco. Didn't get to make it to the top and take pictures." He shoved equipment back in its cases. "Get to do it all over again."

"I'm sorry. But you've been a big help, Oscar. Thank you. And I'll reward you with the cocktails of your choice while we dance in the square tonight."

He growled but gave her a weak smile.

Lucy returned to the table and told Fausta her tale. "If you'll let me know how I can reach you I'll contact you when we're ready to film you."

Fausta hadn't been happy when she heard the news of the broken camera, but cheered when Lucy offered to reach her later. She wrote her phone number on a cocktail napkin.

Lucy smiled at her and reached out to shake her hand. "Chatting with you has been fascinating, and I'm sure your part in our show will be very interesting for our viewers."

When Fausta began her trek across the square, she strutted like a peacock. A peacock in bright pink ankle boots.

"I'm confused," Carrie said after Fausta left. They remained at the table, sipping the only beverage left—water. "What was all of that about where Aurelia used to work? What difference does that make?"

Lucy was twisting a cocktail napkin into a tight spiral, all her attention directed at it. "Let's just say, I think it's interesting that it sounds like Aurelia left her job for an apprenticeship about the same time that she likely got pregnant. Here in Italy, I'm sure that was, and maybe still is, the way unmarried pregnant women did things. They went 'away' for a while. And Aurelia did indeed become a proficient lacemaker, so perhaps she really did use her time there learning the art."

"And Fausta did mention that Aurelia hated her job," Hester added, a touch of a question in her words.

"Yeah, but you know that could have been the excuse for her departure," Lucy said. "She might have told everyone that she was leaving because she hated her job." She rocked her head one way then the other. "As good a cover story as any."

Carrie poured herself more water. "But what difference does any of this make? It doesn't tell us anything about the painting or about who killed her."

Lucy studied Carrie's face as she thought. "No, it doesn't. But there's something about it that feels important. I can only think of two things in Aurelia's life that could have led to her murder. First, the painting and everything associated with it. And second, her secret pregnancy. Both were secrets that she kept from most people. Secrets can lead to violent acts. Or at least the attempt to keep the secrets can."

"What about Enzo? And for that matter, Fausta?" Hester asked sharply.

"Yes, of course they are prime suspects, but they also could be part of those other two turning points in Aurelia's life. Fausta knew about the Nazis. Which means Enzo did too. They had multiple reasons to want Aurelia gone."

"You think the police are looking at them?" Carrie asked.

"Enzo, yes. Fausta I'm not so sure about. If I need some information from Deputy Inspector Maria, I can give her Fausta's name in exchange."

Hester looked taken aback. "What? Don't you think it's your civic duty to tell the police about Fausta now?"

Lucy casually shrugged one shoulder and cocked a brow.

When Hester glared at her in return, Lucy said, "If it starts to look like Fausta really is a suspect, I'll let Maria know."

From the look on Hester's face, Lucy knew this hadn't placated her.

Lucy smiled at her friends. "Change of filming plans, ladies. Tomorrow we head back to Burano to film at the lace museum."

"When did that change?" Carrie asked. "I've been preparing for the shopping in Venice voice-overs."

"It changed about five minutes ago, sorry. But you know the script for the museum. You'll be great."

"What do you have up your sleeve, Lucy?" Hester asked in a tone reeking of suspicion.

"I was feeling bad about not going back to check on Signora Di Votti. You know how much she cared for Aurelia. I'm sure she's having a tough time of it."

Two pairs of eyes glowered at Lucy.

"You don't think I can be nice?"

This earned Lucy a sneer from Carrie and hangdog face from Hester.

"Oh, I know how nice you are, Lucy. You've always been wonderful to me." Hester said, her voice breaking. "I don't mean that I doubt you want to comfort Signora Di Votti. It's just that, you know, I, uh, we, wonder if you're also looking for some information."

"I can do both, you know."

Hester blinked away threatening tears. "I know. Of course, I know you can."

"Don't worry, Hester. I have no ill intentions. However, I do have an errand I want to run, so if I can meet you two later for dinner? Then we have our evening in the square to look forward to." The enthusiasm in her last words changed the mood at the table.

Relieved that everyone was happy again, Lucy dashed off, hoping she could find her way to her destination without Hester's help.

The Questura was about as far from where they were as it could be and still be on the same group of tiny islands.

Lucy ended up taking a vaporetto that went all the way down the Grand Canal to the area where the Questura was located. It was a stunningly beautiful trip, floating past all of the old, majestic buildings, but a slow trip. There were several vaporetto stops along the way, with hordes of people getting on and off at each. It also was a crowded trip—the standing-room-only boat was packed like human sardines in a tin.

By the time she disembarked, Lucy could feel the trickles of sweat weaving their way down her back. Her hair was damp with perspiration. She didn't want to know how she looked.

Once at the Questura building, she breezed through security, and told the officer covering the reception desk that she had an appointment with *Vice Ispettore* Lazzara. Lucy had texted the detective from the vaporetto, requesting a short meeting, which she was granted. The officer understood her and directed her, in excellent English, to Lazzara's office.

Maria Lazzara, wearing a sharp gray suit and pale blue blouse, stood in front of her office talking to another detective when Lucy arrived. Without stopping their conversation, Lazzara waved Lucy into her office.

The small office had a window that was opened to the warm afternoon air. It wasn't uncomfortable, but Lucy wouldn't have minded a bit of air conditioning to cool her overheated body. She sat in the chair in front of the desk, giving her tired feet a break.

When Lazzara walked in Lucy stood to greet her.

The two women exchanged uncomfortable greetings— Lazzara asked how she was enjoying her visit to Venice. Lucy asked how the Carotti case was going.

When that was all out of the way Lucy said, "Are you familiar with the term *quid pro quo*?"

Lazzara sneered. She walked around the desk and sat down. "Of course. And do you know that the term is Latin? A language with its roots right here in my country?"

One point to Maria, Lucy thought. She lowered herself into the chair.

"Of course. I meant no disrespect. I simply wanted to ask you something about the case, and I also have something I've come across that you might be interested in."

Lucy decided Maria Lazzara would have made an excellent poker player. Her face showed nothing about the hand she held or what her next play might have been.

Only after several uncomfortable seconds ticked by, did she ask, "What is the information you have to share?"

Lucy knew there was no way she was going to get away with demanding the information she wanted before she gave up hers.

"I saw Aurelia's husband, Enzo, with a woman. I spoke with the woman. She has an interesting story. Her name is Fausta Patela. Have you come across her?"

Maria blinked once. "No. Who is she?"

"Enzo's lover. And Aurelia's sister-in-law."

She let that soak in for a moment before she added, "Fausta is married to Aurelia's brother. And she's Enzo's lover. And according to her, everyone in the little foursome knew about Enzo and Fausta."

Maria picked up a pen and drew small, concentric circles on a legal pad. Lucy waited patiently for her to digest this information.

"I'll pass this along to the Chief Inspector."

Lucy nodded.

"I was wondering if you could tell me about the payments Aurelia made to Laura. Do you know when they started?"

Maria began doodling again. "I think about three months ago. Three payments had been made."

Keeping her own poker face firmly in place, Lucy simply said, "Okay. Thank you."

Lucy got up, wished Maria a good day, and left the office with the information she had desired.

~ twenty two ~

O
F THEIR FOURSOME, ONLY CARRIE shared in Lucy's enthusiasm for an evening of dancing in the square. Despite Lucy's many descriptions of the atmosphere, the music, the sheer beauty of the experience, neither Hester nor Oscar seemed terribly moved. However, they'd agreed to go, and there was no way Lucy was going to let them out of that agreement. Besides, she'd told them, the experience would make for an evocative article in their magazine. Getting feedback from all three of them would help to add some interesting layers to the story.

Together, in Lucy's room, Carrie and Lucy prepared for the evening. Lucy had no need to wow anyone—after all Nicolo would be performing at La Fenice—but she did want to look presentable. Carrie helped her with her hair and after much badgering on Carrie's part, allowed her to apply the smaller false eyelashes.

Lucy wore the same dress she wore the night Nicolo took her to the square, and Carrie wore a full-skirted sundress with a short, quarter sleeve cardigan.

Dressed and put together, the two women then headed to Hester's room, ostensibly to pick her up for their evening adventures, but in reality to make sure she wasn't wearing anything dour.

It was a nervous looking Hester who opened her door. Hester had skipped her high school prom for fear of having to dance, so Lucy could appreciate her anxiety about dancing in the *piazza*. Of course, had Oscar asked her to the prom, she might have gone. She just wouldn't have danced. But that was all to stop here in Venice.

Though she may have been nervous, Hester had pulled out all the stops when she'd dressed. She wore a slinky, pale gray dress with an asymmetrical hemline. The dress hugged every perfect curve of her body. If Oscar didn't try to dance with her straight away, some other man in the *piazza* certainly would. As usual, her hair was down and casual and sexier than either Lucy or Carrie could have pulled off regardless of how much they worked at it. Lucy had a brief moment of hatred for her best friend, knowing that Hester most likely had done nothing to her hair save a quick run of her fingers through the blond mane.

"You look gorgeous," Carrie told Hester with enthusiasm.

"You sure do," Lucy echoed. "Let's get going, though. Oscar will be waiting for us in the lobby."

"Thank you," Hester said modestly. "You two look lovely as well."

Lucy grabbed her arm and moved her toward the door. "Now, don't go getting all worried about this evening. It's going to be fun. A once in a lifetime experience."

The trio found Oscar waiting impatiently in the lobby.

"Whoa," Carrie squealed when she saw him. "You brought your A game, dude! I like it!"

Oscar, who rolled his eyes and shook his head dismissively, wore black slacks with a slim-fitting wine colored shirt. It was a decidedly European look.

Lucy secretly cheered. Both Hester and Oscar looked as if they were set to enjoy the evening.

Just as when Lucy had danced with Nicolo, the square looked like a fairyland. The lights on the basilica exaggerated the already magical quality of the glorious church. Sitting at one end of the square, it beckoned visitors in at least as much as the music did.

Lucy, exceedingly aware that the evening required a delicate touch, suggested a stroll around the *piazza* before they settled into dancing.

Hester appeared to be relieved by this plan.

Carrie, however, waved it off. "Nope. See that handsome man standing to the right of the bandstand? I'm going to go ask him to dance."

And she was off.

The other three stared at her as she skipped through the crowds.

A moment later she was leading the man out onto the square and into her arms as they began to dance to a popular song, sung in Italian by a pretty blond woman.

"One down," Lucy muttered to herself.

She led Hester and Oscar on a slow stroll, first in the direction of St. Mark's, then back toward the dancers. There were even more people dancing on this evening then there had been when she had been there with Nicolo.

The song Carrie had been dancing to ended and the band began to play *Lady in Red*. Lucy deemed this a perfect first dance piece of music.

She took Hester's right arm and Oscar's left. "There you go. Perfect dance music." She pulled them toward one another as they both looked shell-shocked.

"What? Huh?" Hester stammered.

"Uh, I don't know," Oscar mumbled.

"Have fun you two!" Lucy waved them off.

Lucy found it painful to watch them move toward one another, away from each other, then stumble back into the general vicinity of one another. She thought she would scream before Oscar finally, gingerly, took Hester in his arms. Even from where she stood she could see Hester chewing on her lips as she kept as much distance as physically possible between herself and Oscar.

However, when two minutes into the dance Oscar pulled Hester closer, Lucy beamed. When he guided Hester further into the cluster of dancers in front of the bandstand, Lucy lost sight of them.

She sighed. Perhaps her work was done for the night.

She scanned the area for Carrie and finally saw her—still with the same man. He looked, to Lucy, like a good dancer. Carrie had done well in choosing him.

An elderly man sitting alone at a cafe table caught Lucy's

eye. She marched over to him, held out her hand, and asked him to dance. His beaming smile warmed her heart, and for the next five minutes he led her in some generic, nameless dance that happened to keep perfectly to the rhythm of the music.

When the music ended, he thanked her profusely in a language Lucy couldn't immediately identify, though she thought it could be Swiss.

After returning him to his table, Lucy turned around and nearly bumped into Carrie, whose broad grin nearly matched the old man's when Lucy had asked him to dance.

"You know what, Lucy? Sometimes you come up with a few good ideas. And this was probably one of the best ever."

The music started up again. This time it was an old big band song. Lucy unconsciously tapped a toe.

"Having fun, I take it?" Lucy asked.

"Oh yeah. I haven't danced in ages. And I've never danced in Piazza San Marco, obviously." She sighed loudly, one hand over her heart.

"I only hope Hester and Oscar are having fun. They didn't come back when that last number ended."

Carrie gave Lucy a sly smile. "Nope. They went straight into the next dance. I was near them. Saw them."

"Were they dancing like robots?"

"Shockingly, no. They looked comfortable. Like anyone else out there dancing."

"Hmmm, whaddya know?"

A female singer stepped to the front of the stage, singing the old Sinatra classic with a sultry Italian accent.

Carrie held out a hand. "Let's dance. We shouldn't waste a classic like this one."

The women danced an energetic Swing dance that could have made a great workout in any gym class. The music transported Lucy back to what she imagined would be World War Two days, though it occurred to her that she might not have wanted to be in this square, in this city, in this country during that particular period of time.

Her train of thought brought her straight back to Aurelia and the stories about her family that Fausta had shared. She mused on the fact that Aurelia had been making payments to Laura. Had the financial burden driven Aurelia to look into selling the painting? Led her to the accountant, Oliveto, to help her sell it on the black market?

She allowed herself two minutes of murder case thinking then shoved the thoughts aside.

The song came to its last notes, leaving Lucy and Carrie breathing hard.

"We should probably do that more often," Lucy suggested. "Good workout."

Carrie shrugged. "Meh. Dancing is only for fun. It should never be thought of as exercise. Takes all the fun out of it."

The band began playing a much slower piece. "I think I'm going to take a turn around the square," Carrie said with a slight waggle of her brows.

"Have fun," Lucy sang to her.

Lucy watched the dancers as she swayed to the music. A smile touched her lips as she remembered the night before.

With Nicolo. Under the stars. Under the watchful eyes of St. Mark.

Carrie's arrival at her side surprised Lucy.

"Hey, I was sure you'd have found another dance partner. What are you doing back so soon?"

Carrie's face was the embodiment of the cat that swallowed the canary. "I saw Hester. And Oscar."

"Okay…"

"I happened to see them through an empty space on the square."

"Okay…"

"Hester looked down at Oscar."

"Of course. She's a little taller than he is. No big deal."

"Then she kissed him."

Lucy's eyes grew huge. "What?" Hester initiating a kiss with the man she'd been secretly in love with since she was fourteen years old could only be likened to some rare astronomical event. A comet that only flies past the solar system once every hundred years. Or the near miss of an asteroid.

"Yes, you heard correctly."

"And?"

"When she pulled her head up, Oscar looked like he was in need of C.P.R."

"I can well imagine. Well, good for her. At long, long, *long* last."

"I wouldn't get our hopes up yet. Neither has had any romantic experience in their forty-five years of life, so this isn't going to be smooth sailing, certainly."

"Good point."

When the music ended, the band took a break. Silence hung uncomfortably over the square. As if the music had been a blanket, Lucy suddenly felt the evening chill and shivered.

Carrie and Lucy strolled toward the bandstand, and when they were just a few yards from it, they ran into Oscar and Hester. Neither was looking at the other. No one was talking. Oscar was shuffling his feet and keeping his eyes on the stones beneath his feet.

"Hi," Lucy said, with false cheer. "Did you have fun dancing?"

Hester smiled shyly. "It is lovely out here, isn't it?"

"That isn't exactly an answer, but I will agree with you. It is lovely," Lucy said.

"And you, Oscar?" Carrie nudged him with her elbow. "Fun time?"

His lips formed a fine line. His eyes narrowed. "Oh…sure. Certainly interesting, I'll give you that."

"So, we have one lovely. One interesting. I suppose that's better than nothing," Lucy said, her eyes meeting Carrie's.

"We have an early start tomorrow," Oscar pointed out. "Maybe we should call it a night."

Lucy tipped her head to one side.

"I'll go for calling it a night if you three will promise me we will all come back one more time before we leave Venice for a full evening of dancing."

Oscar stared blankly at Lucy. Hester's face took on a peachy tint, but she smiled and agreed it was a fair idea.

"Well, you know I'm all in," Carrie enthused.

"Excellent. It's a plan, then."

The group started toward the far end of the square where they could exit. Oscar took the lead—a lead that increased the closer they got to the hotel. Carrie and Hester walked arm in arm behind him.

And Lucy took up the rear as she softly sang, *Santa Lucia*.

∼ twenty three ∼

A CERTAIN TENSION HUNG IN the air as the group traveled to Burano. Tension that arose from a slight change in the axis of their friendships. Until Hester and Oscar found their footing in their changed world, nothing would feel quite right among the four of them.

Lucy was delighted by the lack of equilibrium.

At long last, the heavy secret had been exposed.

Though the whole situation felt much more like something a person would experience in high school, not when they were forty-five.

As the water taxi skimmed along the lagoon water in the glaring early morning sun, neither Oscar nor Hester could bring themselves to make eye contact with the other. Lucy kept a vigilant eye on them. She found it difficult not to grin.

It was a quiet trip. The only words spoken were quickly whispered conversations that Lucy had with Carrie. But they were brief, as Lucy needed to monitor the Hester/Oscar situation.

When the boat finally docked at Burano, an hour after

leaving San Marco, Oscar hurried ahead of the other three, carrying his camera equipment to the lace museum.

"Carrie," Lucy said in a full voice, the first word spoken out loud since leaving Venice. "You have your script. Why don't you go ahead with Oscar." Out of Hester's line of vision, Lucy winked at Carrie. "Hester and I have some other research we need to take care of."

Lucy could feel Hester's relief when she heard that she wouldn't need to be in close proximity to Oscar. Carrie gave Lucy a wry smile.

"Sounds good," Carrie sang as she skipped away to follow in Oscar's wake.

Turning to Hester, Lucy said, "Do you mind helping me with a chat I'd like to have with Signora Di Votti?"

"Of course. Maybe we could take a stroll around the island, too. We didn't get to do that the last time we were here."

"Good idea. I'd say we could probably see the entire island in, oh, say, about ten minutes." Lucy laughed at the truth of the statement, and after a momentary lag Hester joined in.

"Those two will be busy for at least an hour and a half or more likely two hours, so let's visit Di Votti and then we can relax and enjoy ourselves." Lucy knew this news would help dissipate Hester's remaining anxiety.

When they reached the lace shop where Aurelia had been employed Hester started for the door, but Lucy grabbed her elbow.

"Just a sec, I'd like to walk to the end of this canal before we go in," Lucy explained, guiding Hester back to the canal.

She wanted to make sure her memory wasn't flawed, and that a dock and a refueling area did indeed sit at the far end of the canal.

They hadn't gone far when Lucy could see the lagoon and wooden pilings rising out of it.

When they reached the lagoon, everything was as she had assumed. There was a place to fuel-up boats, and a few spots to dock vessels. It would make the perfect place to park a boat, strangle someone who was expecting to meet them, throw the body in the canal, and then speed off in their boat, back into the lagoon to any one of the myriad of little islands that dotted the area.

Lucy also knew that any police detective worth his or her salt would recognize this possibility, and she was sure the detective in charge of the case would have investigated it.

But she needed to double-check for her own satisfaction.

Hester didn't ask what they were doing in the most unsavory place on Burano, which told Lucy where her mind was.

"Come on. Let's go talk to our friendly lace lady," Lucy said cheerily.

Zombie Hester followed without question.

Signora Di Votti wasn't posted at her usual spot outside despite the presence of at least a dozen browsing tourists checking out the wares, so Lucy stepped inside. The little space, packed tightly with lace and linen items was also full of shoppers. While it had been busy on their previous visit, it wasn't anything like this.

Lucy knew that the murder had brought gawkers, more than it had brought shoppers.

A steady stream of people climbed and descended the stairs to Aurelia's old workspace.

Behind the counter with its old-fashioned cash register, stood Signora Di Votti.

Lucy got in line. There were two buying customers in front of her.

"Hester, would you please grab some napkins or something else not too expensive?"

Hester didn't ask why, but simply did what she was told. Less than a minute later she handed Lucy two white napkins with an edging of machine-made lace. Lucy checked the price. Fifteen euros each. That was acceptable.

When Lucy's turn came, Signora Di Votti glanced up at her without any sign of recognition. She began to ring up the sale, then her head jerked up, and her mouth dropped open.

"Ah, Signora Lucy!" She reached across the counter and grabbed both of Lucy's hands. "How good to see you." Without dropping Lucy's hands, she turned around and called over her shoulder to someone. To Lucy, she said, "You wait. I come out."

When a young woman from the back arrived to take over the counter Signora Di Votti joined Lucy and Hester.

"Let us go out. In the back."

They followed the woman outside to the narrow *calle* where they had chatted with Signora Di Votti on the day Aurelia was killed.

"They have not discovered the man who killed my Aurelia," a despairing Signora Di Votti reported after greeting Hester.

"We know," Lucy told her. "And I'm trying to help them find the killer. I was wondering if you could help me by telling me about Aurelia when she first started working here. How long ago was that?"

"I help you. Yes," she said emphatically. She looked down at her hands and started touching the fingers of her left hand with the forefinger of her right, her lips moving as she did so. She repeated this a few times.

Signora Di Votti nodded. "Yes. She start here almost eighteen years ago."

Hester rested a hand on the woman's upper arm. "That's a long time. I can see why she was like a daughter to you."

Di Votti pressed her lips together. Her fingers played with a silver cross necklace.

"Do you know what Aurelia did before she began her lace-making career?" Lucy asked gently.

Signora Di Votti squinted as if searching the past. "*Si,* I do. She worked in an…office. Uh, secretary?"

"Okay. Do you happen to know what the business was? Or what kind of business it was?"

"Uh, how you say…selling things to other countries?"

"Export?" Lucy tried to verify that they were talking about the same thing.

"Yes. That. Export."

"Do you remember the name? Or maybe you have the name in a personnel file on Aurelia?"

"I don't know if in a file. Old files, more than ten year are kept at home. But maybe I will remember."

Lucy gave her a gentle smile. "If you happen to remember or can find it in a file that would be very helpful. Did you ever know any of her friends from that time?"

This made the woman grin broadly. "Oh yes! Her best friend. She apprenticed at same time with same woman as Aurelia, and they come to Burano together."

Lucy and Hester exchanged a quick, optimistic glance.

Lucy held her breath as she said, "Do you remember her name?"

The previously grave, pensive Signora Di Votti clapped her hands together and laughed.

"Oh, *si, si*! She lives on Burano still. Martina Napoli. She does lace at the Museo del Merletto. She there now."

Lucy threw her arms around Signora Di Votti and hugged her in a moment of spontaneous relief.

Finally, someone who could shed light on Aurelia's past.

"Signora, thank you so much! *Grazie*!" Lucy sang. "This is very helpful. And I will let you know if I find out anything that will help me find Aurelia's killer."

Di Votti said something in Italian. The emotion was easily translated, but for the meaning, Lucy turned to Hester.

"It's a prayer," Hester told her. "She's blessing your efforts to find the killer."

Lucy met Signora Di Votti's eyes and said, "Thank you. I need the prayer. Please keep praying that we find the person who did this to Aurelia."

Tears welled up in the woman's eyes. She hugged Lucy, then Hester. They said their goodbyes and went back inside the shop, where Signora Di Votti went back to work. Lucy and Hester made their way through the busy place and on out to the square.

"I hope you don't mind if we put off the stroll about the island," Lucy said. "I'd like to get back to the museum and find this Martina."

"Me too," Hester readily agreed. "Do you think this will help?"

"I do," Lucy said as she set a quick pace back to the museum.

"May I ask why? Why you think that time in Aurelia's life is important to her murder?"

"I'm not sure, actually. But lately, there's been a lot that's pointed to the time when she gave up her son to be adopted. It feels important."

"But what about the painting?"

"I think it's part of this too. I just haven't figured out how."

The trip back to the museum only took a couple of minutes. Had they run they could have been there in thirty seconds, the island is so small.

They approached the door, and Lucy grabbed Hester's wrist.

"You going to be okay in there?" Lucy asked, her brows raised in question.

Hester looked off to the side of Lucy. "Of course." The words didn't convince Lucy.

"I would say you could stay out here, but I might need you to translate."

"I'm fine. Really."

"Okay. I know that everything is kind of awkward right now. But it will get better. I promise." *And it would help if either of you were in tune with your feelings*, Lucy thought, rather uncharitably.

Hester gave her a tight smile. "I'm sure you're right."

"Come on. We have a lace-maker to find!"

Finding Martina Napoli was no problem. Extricating her from the tourists crowded around her oohing and awing at her nimble fingers creating lace…that was a little trickier.

When Lucy finally had success at removing Martina from the museum, she and Hester led her to a table outside. They sat down, Martina looking puzzled over what was going on. When she'd heard the name *Aurelia,* she got up from her station and followed the two American women.

Martina Napoli was a petite woman in her mid-thirties, with long, thick, dark hair and eyes that matched her hair. She wore a simple blue dress with a large lace collar. The other two lacemakers wore similar outfits—Lucy assumed it was the required attire for the job.

"Do you speak English?" Lucy asked, carefully pronouncing each word slowly.

"A little. More than I did five years ago." She giggled.

"Thank you for talking to us. My name is Lucy, and this is my friend, Hester. We are trying to help the police find the person who killed your friend, Aurelia."

Lucy had barely gotten the last word out of her mouth when Martina covered her face and began to sob. Hester caught Lucy's eye and grimaced.

Lucy decided it was best to allow Martina a moment to cry. She knew nothing would be accomplished until the poor woman could get it out of her system.

A few minutes later Martina drew a lace-edged handkerchief out of a pocket and wiped her face.

In a quavering voice, she said, "I am sorry. Aurelia was my best friend. I miss her. Very much."

"Of course you do," Hester said softly, her brows knitted in empathy.

"You say you are trying to find her killer?"

"Yes," Lucy assured her.

"I will help however I can."

"Thank you, Martina. First, we got your name from Signora Di Votti, whom we met on the day Aurelia...died. We know she cared very much for Aurelia and I wanted to let her know we were trying to help."

"This is so kind of you."

Lucy's mouth turned up in a grim smile.

"We want to help. I heard that you knew Aurelia for many years." Lucy nodded encouragement.

"Yes. Many years. We learned lace together."

Lucy knew she was about to take a big risk, but there was no avoiding it if she had any hope of discovering what was needed.

"Martina, I know that Aurelia had a baby about that time.

Was she pregnant when you were in your apprenticeship together?"

Martina's eyes widened in alarm and flickered from Lucy to Hester and back.

"It is okay, you can tell us. It might help us find her killer."

Martina twisted the handkerchief and chewed on her lower lip. Finally, she nodded.

"Did she ever mention anything about the father?"

She cast her eyes down at her hands and shook her head.

"No, she wouldn't talk about him. I never asked."

"I understand. Maybe, did she ever talk about the job she had that she hated so much?"

Martina let out a loud guffaw. "Oh yes! She hated the office. So much she did. Never wanted to work in an office again."

"Do you happen to know where she worked? The name of the business?"

"She worked in a part of the office that did…the money. The money in and money out."

"You mean the accounting office?"

Martina's face brightened. "*Sì*! Accounting."

"Martina, I know this was a long time ago, but do you happen to remember any of the names of the people she worked with?"

She pursed her lips. Lucy didn't say anything while she seemed to be searching her memory.

"Well, let's do it this way. Do you remember if she worked with women? Or men? Or both?"

"I remember that. One woman—she liked her. Two men—and she did not like them." Her eyes blazed as she mentioned the men.

"This is good, Martina. Very helpful." Lucy gently encouraged her, hoping to help her wend her way through her memories.

Lucy knew only too well the danger of inadvertently planting a false memory, but she was getting desperate. Giovanni's forlorn face flashed through her mind.

"Martina, I'm going to say a name, and if it sounds familiar, please let me know." She waited for Martina to acknowledge the plan. When she did, Lucy said, "Alberti."

Martina jerked like she'd been hit with several volts of electricity.

"Yes! Wait…" She held up a hand, palm facing Lucy and Hester. Seconds ticked by.

"Alberti Oliveto!" She slapped the table in triumph.

In a noisy exhalation, Lucy let out the breath she'd been holding.

"Oh, Martina, this could be so helpful. Thank you, thank you. I think this will help us find Aurelia's killer."

"You think this man knows something?"

"I think so. I think he might have information about Aurelia that would help us find the killer."

Hester, who was the most intelligent person Lucy had ever known or was likely to know, stared dumbly at Lucy and Martina in turns. Lucy knew Hester's quick mind would catch up soon enough.

"Martina, I'm going to leave you my card." Lucy placed

a card on the table in front of Martina. "If you remember anything else, anything at all, please call me."

Lucy made a move to get up but quickly sat back down.

"When was the last time you spoke to Aurelia?"

"Just the day before she was…uh…died."

"Was there something that had been bothering her before she died?"

"I thought so. She seemed not right. But she didn't say."

"Do you know if she was having money problems?"

Lucy could see Aurelia's best friend weigh the benefits of keeping her friend's confidences versus helping to find her killer.

Finally, she said, "Yes. But she said they would be over soon. She had a plan."

"Do you know what that plan was?"

"No. But she said something strange once."

When she didn't continue, Lucy encouraged her. "It's okay. It won't hurt Aurelia now. It will only help."

She nodded. "I know. It is just so…strange talking about her like this."

Hester leaned in. "I'm sure it is. Lucy is my best friend, and I can imagine what it would be like to be in your place. But I know Aurelia would want you to help."

"Yes." She took a deep breath. "She said, just a week or two ago, that she had her dead *nona* to thank for getting her out of money problem."

"*Nona*, grandmother, right?"

"*Si*, yes."

Lucy exchanged a look with Hester.

"We shouldn't keep you away from your work any longer. But, Martina, you have been so helpful. Thank you. I will keep in touch if I learn something more, and don't forget to call me if you remember anything."

"I will."

They stood, and Martina pulled Lucy into a hug.

"*Grazie, grazie!*" Martina clung to Lucy.

"I think we will find the person," Lucy reassured Martina while the little Italian woman nearly squeezed the life out of her.

When she finally released her, Lucy watched as she went back into the museum.

A tear surprised Lucy as it popped from her eye. Another, from the other eye, quickly followed it.

She took the one step separating her from Hester and threw her arms around her.

Hester initially stiffened at the unexpected embrace, but seconds later relaxed.

"I know," she said into Lucy's hair. "I can't imagine losing you either."

Lucy released her and gave herself a little shake.

"Let's take that stroll, now, shall we?"

Hester grinned at her. "Excellent idea! Maybe we could find an espresso?"

"And a pastry!" Lucy cheered. For some reason, an extra bit of weight didn't seem all that important right then.

~ twenty four ~

B Y THE TIME THEY ARRIVED back in Venice shortly
after noon, the Italian sun was blazing, and the
temperature had become uncomfortably hot. After
consulting with Hester, Lucy gave everyone the afternoon
off, with the plan that they would do some sunset shots when
it might be cooler.

And an afternoon off gave Lucy time to think through
everything she'd recently learned about Aurelia and the case.

On a large piece of chart paper she'd dug out of the
supply duffel, Lucy began noting everything she deemed
important to the case. She arranged her notes in a large web,
with lines connecting bits of information that seemed
connected.

Then she called Hester and asked her to join her in her
room for an investigation debriefing.

With no air conditioning, the room was warm, but Lucy
had opened the large windows, and the air moved through
the room. She'd changed into a sundress and was barefoot,
the classic Venetian flooring cool on her feet.

By the time Hester arrived, Lucy had taped the chart paper to the mirror that hung over the desk.

"You look cool and more comfortable," Hester commented when she saw Lucy's bare feet and dress. Then her eye was drawn to the chart, and she made her way over to it. "Wow, you've been busy."

"Yep. Have a seat." Lucy waved at the chair that sat a few feet in front of its desk. "Let me run you through some of the things I know about the case, and some of the inferences I'm making based on that information. I know you'll be able to catch anything I'm getting wrong."

Hester simply nodded. She may have been self-deprecating about many things, but her intellect was never one of them.

"First, as an introduction, let me explain that this web is based on a principle that I've found to be true in most crimes. You know, from my years of crime analysis. And just life in general, I guess." Lucy tipped her head to one side, considering the truth of this. "So, often when a person becomes a victim, something in their life has changed prior to the crime. Like, say, a person's home might be burglarized after the owner changes from night shift to day shift. No one home at night, burglar takes advantage of that. Or a woman might be the victim of domestic violence after her husband loses his job."

Hester nodded her understanding.

"So I looked at what had changed in Aurelia's life. First, she left her husband, and she knew he was cheating on her with her sister-in-law." Lucy pointed to the word,

Aurelia, in the center of the web, and then at *Leaves Enzo/cheating.*

"Do you think one of them did it? Or both?"

"I do think it is a possibility. Except that there was a bigger change in her life just a few months ago."

She tapped the words *Giovanni arrives.* "The son she birthed eighteen years ago suddenly showed up. And no, I don't think he killed her. There's no motive for him to do so."

Lucy ran a finger over the line that connected Giovanni's arrival with *Laura.* "But..." she sang. "About the time her son showed up, she began making payments to her roommate, Laura. The timing is too right on the mark to be a coincidence. I think Laura found out about Giovanni and either started blackmailing Aurelia, or Aurelia offered her money to keep her mouth shut. No one knew about the baby she'd given up. Except for Martina. Aurelia would have wanted to keep it that way."

"But didn't Fausta say she'd known Aurelia all their lives? Maybe she knew."

Lucy stared at the web, tapping a finger on her lips. "And how would that work in with a motive for Fausta—or Enzo—to kill her?"

"Well, clearly, it would have behooved them to be rid of her. Let's say, Fausta found out that Giovanni came back. She went to Aurelia asking for money. Then she killed her..." Hester shook her head. "Never mind. You don't kill someone before you get the money."

"And how do we know she didn't get the money?"

"The painting was still here. She hadn't gotten any money for it yet."

"What if Fausta knew about the painting? Figured she and Enzo could get rid of Aurelia and then take the painting?"

Hester's eyes grew large. "Oh, my. That makes sense."

Lucy looked at her web. She took a marker and drew a line from Fausta/Enzo to the painting.

"You know what? This wasn't what I'd intended to say. I was going to draw the web from Giovanni to Aurelia and someone she knew around the time she worked at the infamous office."

"Where would that lead you?"

Lucy rubbed her face, and then massaged her temples. "I don't know!" she said, exasperation in her voice. "Wherever it was, now I'm thinking this Fausta and the painting thing makes a lot more sense."

Lucy threw herself onto the bed.

"Now I'm just confused. Maybe I should give up for now and take a nap," Lucy groaned.

"Would you like some time on your own? I might go sit by the window in my room and read."

"Yeah, that sounds nice. You should do that. I might take a slow-motion walk through some shady *calli*. Get a cold drink. Or a gelato. Clear my fuzzy head."

Hester stood and smiled warmly at Lucy. "You'll get it. I don't doubt it for an instant."

Lucy appreciated the sincere belief in her abilities.

She only wished she shared them.

Hester left and Lucy slipped on comfortable walking sandals. She grabbed her purse and sunglasses and headed out into the hot Italian sun.

Lucy had been walking down various *calli* not far from the hotel for a good fifteen minutes before it occurred to her that it might have been a good idea to take note of all of the turns she took.

Getting back to the hotel could prove to be difficult and it was too hot to get oneself comfortably lost.

It was time for that cold drink. Lucy wondered for the first time in the week she'd been in Venice if anyone on the island made iced tea.

She ducked into a little trattoria and asked the girl at the counter about the possibility of iced tea.

The girl appeared confused by the request.

"Do you speak English?"

"Yes. You want something cold to drink?" Lucy didn't think she imagined the shock on the girl's face.

"Well, yes. It's hot out. I'd like something cold."

"Huh, Americans." She shook her head in amusement. "We have tea in a bottle. Okay?"

"Okay. But why is this an American thing?"

"You like cold drinks when it is hot," she said over her shoulder as she reached under the counter.

Lucy looked askance at the girl.

She handed Lucy a cold bottle of iced tea. "Here we do hot when hot, cold when cold."

Lucy was sorely tempted to say something that could begin a culture war, so she bit her tongue instead, paid for the tea, and turned to leave.

She hadn't made it to the door, though, when she heard her name called out from the back of the trattoria.

Turning around, she saw a grinning Giovanni.

"Hi!" she said, genuinely happy to see him.

He hurried over to her.

"Can you wait minuto? I will come out. We can talk."

"Sure."

Lucy stepped outside and waited for Giovanni by the door.

When he came out, he led the way a few doors down to a tiny shop that sold sandwiches and slices of pizza. It was like Giovanni's shop, only smaller.

"I think you like here. It has cool air."

Lucy did indeed feel the cooler air the moment she walked in. She sent a prayer of thanks for air conditioning to the heavens.

"Thank you. This feels good."

They sat down at one of the barstools in the window, though they didn't order anything. Lucy was tempted to ask how he was going to get away with this but decided to keep her mouth shut for a change.

As they'd walked down the *calle*, Lucy remembered the day when she'd walked down a similar *calle* and had experienced a sensation of being watched and followed. She peered at Giovanni.

"I must ask you something, Giovanni. Did you follow me a few days ago?"

He chewed on his lips and examined a fingernail. "*Si*. I so sorry. I thought you know something."

She nodded and gave him a wan smile. "Yes, that's what I thought." When she saw his pained expression, she quickly added, "Don't worry about it. I understand why you followed me."

Their eyes met. Giovanni whispered, "*Grazie*, for not being…angry."

Lucy gave him a pat on the back.

"You know anything? About my *madre?*" he asked after a few moments of silence, hope now apparent on his face.

"Yes, and no. I don't know who killed Aurelia, but I do have some new information that could be very helpful."

"Oh," he said, downcast.

"But, you know what? I would like to ask you something that I was wondering about after a chat I had with someone who knew your mother. Birth mother." As with her previous conversation with Giovanni, she forced herself to slow down and speak clearly.

His face brightened.

"I spoke to someone who knew Aurelia back when she was pregnant with you." Lucy saw the corners of his mouth twitch in anticipation of a smile. "You told me the other day that she wouldn't tell you who your father was. Did she say anything about why she wouldn't tell you?"

He frowned and shook his head.

"You don't need to rush. Think about it for a minute. Think about any conversations you had with Aurelia."

Lucy watched as he thought about it. She could almost

see him running the videos of his memories with Aurelia.

He began to nod his head slowly, as if to a beat only he could hear. Perhaps his videos had a soundtrack.

"I think I remember. Something. She say…I think she say…my father would not want to know."

Lucy chewed on that for a moment.

Then she asked, "Do you think she meant that he didn't know about you? That she never told him she was pregnant?"

Giovanni shrugged.

"Or…" Lucy began, as a thought percolated to the surface. "Maybe he wouldn't want to know that you had shown up and that she had met you."

"I do not know. Does not make a difference, huh?"

Lucy thought it did make a difference. A difference of about eighteen years. And a difference that could have led to a road that in turn led to murder.

"Lucy…" He spoke the name softly as he looked down at the floor. "Do you think I could meet this person you talk to? Who knew my mother?"

Lucy smiled at Giovanni. "I think she would like that very much." She told Giovanni about Martina and how to find her. "She loved Aurelia. She was her best friend, and she's missing her terribly. Meeting you would be just what she needs right now."

"*Grazie*, Lucy. You will tell me if you find more?"

"Absolutely. And right now I think I'm going to try to find a person who might be able to give me some information I could use. Take care of yourself, Giovanni."

Lucy put an arm around his shoulder and gave it a squeeze.

When she stepped back into the *calle,* the heat blasted her mercilessly. It was a humid heat and she could feel herself grow sticky with perspiration within seconds. The hotel was only a ten-minute walk away, but she knew she'd need a shower as soon as she reached it.

But first, she needed to make a phone call and set up a business dinner date.

She had a sudden need for some accounting services.

~ twenty five ~

LUCY MOVED SLOWLY AS SHE retraced her steps back to the hotel. Her pace was partly due to the heavy, hot air weighing down on her, but it also could have been attributed to the myriad of murder case theories running through her mind.

The two theories she believed had the most credence both led to the same man.

There was no way of solving this crime until she had another talk with Alberti Oliveto. He held the key.

She sent out a group text to Hester, Oscar, and Carrie. What she planned to do she couldn't do on her own.

Lucy had no more than tapped the send button on her text than the phone rang in her hand, causing her to jump.

The number came up with something in Italian as its identification. One word jumped out at her. *Questura*.

"Hello?" There was a definite question in her voice.

"Lucy Tuppence? This is Maria Lazzara."

"Oh. Hello, Signora Lazzara." She carefully didn't ask why she was calling.

"We have some new financial information on the case that I thought you might be interested in."

"Yes, I certainly would be."

"Aurelia Carotti made three bank deposits, once a month for three months. They were all cash deposits. Each for seven hundred and fifty euros."

Lucy took a moment to calm her breathing, which had taken off for the races with Maria's news. "Could you tell me when the first deposit was made?"

"Three months ago. At the end of February."

"Do you have a date?"

"Uh, yeah." Lucy heard her shuffling papers. "That would be February twentieth."

"Interesting that so much was going on in February, isn't it?"

"What do you mean?" Lazarra asked, pointedly.

Lucy suddenly recalled that the police didn't know anything about Giovanni and his recent appearance. At least not as far as Lucy knew.

"Well, didn't she begin making payments to her roommate around that same time?" she asked, all innocence.

"Oh, yes. Of course. It does make for an interesting pattern."

"May I ask if the other payments were also made on the twentieth of the month?"

There was a long pause. Lucy feared she'd taken it a step too far.

"Well…yes, they were. And I'm afraid that is all I can say right now. I just thought you'd like to know about the payments."

"Yes, indeed. I really appreciate it. Thank you for calling."

They simultaneously ended the call.

To the empty hotel room, Lucy said, "Well, well, well, Aurelia, you were a busy woman in February, weren't you?"

Lucy sat on the hotel terrace, awaiting the arrival of her friends. At least she hoped they would show up.

While she waited, she ordered a Spritz Aperol from the tiny bar that sat at one end of the terrace. Now she sat in the shade sipping the sweet, refreshing drink of Venice.

Carrie was the first to arrive. When she saw what Lucy was drinking, she bypassed the table and made a beeline to the bar.

With her own Spritz in her hand, she joined Lucy.

"So, what's up? Travel business or sleuth work?" Carrie sipped the drink.

"Sleuth. I need you guys to work back-up for me."

Carrie cocked a brow and one side of her mouth. "That sounds intriguing. Very cop-like. Working back-up. Whatever it is, you can count me in."

"Thank you. But you might want to wait until you hear the whole thing before you answer. And I'm hoping Oscar and Hester get here soon." Lucy glanced over her shoulder at the door to the terrace. No one was there.

Carrie giggled. "Oscar and Hester. What if…" This time she waggled her perfectly formed brows.

"Yeah, right. If that were the case, we wouldn't be sitting here in the heat, because everything would have frozen over."

"I know. But they were so cute last night." Carrie grinned at the memory.

Their chatter came to an abrupt end when Oscar ambled over to the table. His eye went to the bright orange drinks sitting on the table.

"Spritz o'clock, I see. I'll be right back."

The two women watched as he strode over to the bar, and only when he was clear on the other end of the terrace did they allow themselves to laugh.

"That was close," Carrie stated the obvious.

"A bit."

When Oscar was settled in at the table, sipping his cocktail, Lucy asked, "Have you seen Hester?" The words were delivered with false innocence.

Lucy thought she could see the hint of pink on Oscar's dark complexion. "Uh, no. I don't know where she is." Lucy noted that he didn't make eye contact.

She inhaled deeply. "Look here, Oscar." There was no missing the *I mean business* tone she used. He looked up at her sideways. "Hester has been in love with you since we were all fourteen years old. Give the poor woman a break and make another move. Last night was a great, *great* start. Don't let things hang there now. Move it along."

"In love with me?" His voice squeaked.

"What is wrong with men?" Lucy barked. "Are you blind, Oscar? Yes. Yes, she is in love with you. Now, what are you going to do about it?"

Oscar's eyes had become glassy. His mouth agape. And there was no question that he was blushing.

"I…I…don't know," he stammered. "It's a lot to take in. I mean this is shocking."

"Really?" Carrie nearly shouted. "I don't buy it. You had to know. So what is wrong? Don't you feel a little something for her too?"

Oscar looked shellshocked. "I…I guess. I never really thought about it. I mean, you know, she's *Hester*."

With that one word, Lucy understood everything.

"Oscar, if she's been in love with you all this time, then she doesn't exactly think she's in a different league than you are. She thinks you two are in the exact, same league."

Lucy thought he looked a little green around the gills.

"Take a swallow of your Spritz," she ordered him.

He did as he was told, then blurted, "But she's kind of a kook, you know."

Lucy could see that Carrie was about to explode.

In a carefully measured tone, Lucy said, "Oscar, honey, we all are. Have you never realized this ridiculously obvious fact? Math and science geeks? Chess club enthusiasts? We are all a little on the kooky end of the spectrum." Lucy knew, however, that Hester took it to a new level. There was an absent-minded professor air about her. No one who knew her could deny that.

Oscar examined the liquid in his glass as if he were analyzing the bubble patterns.

No one had the opportunity to say anything more because Hester walked in just then and joined them. If she noticed the heavy silence at the table, she chose not to mention it.

"Hi, Hester," Lucy said cheerily. "Now that we're all here, I'd like to share with you the favor I'm going to ask. If, and that's a big if I'm afraid, everything goes to plan I'm wondering if you could work back-up for me while I meet with a, shall we say, person of interest."

"You know you can always count on me," Hester assured her.

"Thank you, Hester, and Carrie said earlier that she would help too." Lucy turned her focus to Oscar. "Oscar? I could really use you too."

"Tell me what it is exactly."

"Sure. I'm hoping to meet this man in a public place, for safety reasons, and I would like it if you three were nearby. In fact, it would probably be just Carrie, and you, Oscar. I'm hoping Hester will be right with me when I meet the guy."

"I'll be happy to," Hester said. "Who is it?"

"Well, here's the tricky part. You and I have already met him, Hester. The accountant. Remember he said he didn't know Aurelia?"

"Oh yeah."

"Yeah." Lucy turned to Oscar and Carrie. "It turns out he did know her. Hester and I found this out when we were on Burano this morning. We had a conversation with Aurelia's best friend. And I think the accountant's number was in her phone book for one of two reasons."

Three pairs of eyes peered at her.

"I'll tell you later. But, Hester, we're going to have to play our roles carefully. Remember how last time we saw him we told him you were interested in buying a second home, here in Venice?"

Hester nodded.

"This time we're going to play the Nilsson card. When I call him I'm going to tell him who you really are, since your name didn't seem to ring any bells last time we saw him. He'll make sure he does whatever he needs to in order to meet us for dinner tonight."

"That might work," Hester said, a hint of optimism in her voice.

Lucy turned to the recalcitrant Oscar. "And now that you know what we're up to, do you think you can join us?"

Oscar's eyes flickered to Hester.

"Yeah. I'll do it."

"Okay! Wish me luck. I'm going to make that call."

Fifteen minutes later Lucy and Hester had a dinner date with Alberti Oliveto at an outdoor restaurant overlooking the Grand Canal. He had gone for the bait—hook, line, and sinker, anxious to make a client of the immensely wealthy Hester Nilsson.

"We have a few hours before we have to meet him," Lucy told the group. "Let's take some time to relax and prepare."

"I'm going to spend the next three hours in a cool bath," a perspiring Carrie announced, as she fanned herself.

Oscar leaned toward Hester as if to say something, but quickly moved away and got up. Without a word, he left the terrace.

Carrie left for her bath.

"Do you mind staying just a few minutes, so we can go

over what I'm hoping to accomplish tonight?" Lucy asked.

"Of course." She sat up, ready to hear the plan.

Lucy took her time laying out her case. Both of her cases, more accurately, since she was looking at two separate scenarios.

Two scenarios in which Signor Oliveto was the key.

Before they parted, Lucy made one more phone call. Hopefully, the recipient of the call would take her request seriously.

~ twenty six ~

L UCY MADE SURE THEY ARRIVED early for the
meeting. She and Hester were ushered to a table
overlooking the Grand Canal. Lights from ancient
palazzi and boats reflected in the water. The voices of
gondoliers made their way up to the third-floor terrace.
Music from a distant accordion added to the Venetian
ambience.

Lucy found herself wishing she wasn't trying to get
crucial information in a murder case, but instead was
enjoying the venue with Nicolo.

He'd called while she was enjoying a bubble bath before
leaving for this meeting. At the end of their pleasant chat,
they had made plans to meet for lunch the next day.

Perhaps it was due to this phone call that Lucy now
yearned for an entirely different dinner scenario.

Lucy and Hester sat at one table, and Carrie and Oscar
sat at the one directly next to it. They arranged themselves
at their tables so that eye contact would be possible
throughout the meeting. Lucy had ordered a bottle of wine

and was pouring a glass for Hester and one for herself when Signor Oliveto arrived.

Hester stood and held out her hand. After Oliveto shook it, he sat down in the one open seat, eyeing Hester warily as he did so.

"You ladies were at my office the other day."

His eyes shifted from Hester to Lucy and back. "You wanted to use the accountant a friend recommended. Now, this makes no difference?"

Hester met his gaze. "I had my people look into you and the firm you work for," she lied. "You appear to have an excellent reputation. If this meeting goes well, I think I will be contracting with you to take care of my Venice financial needs. And I'd like you to meet my vice president of personnel, Lucy Tuppence."

Lucy gave him a curt nod. She was impressed with how professionally Hester delivered her speech. But then, she reminded herself, Hester does oversee the running a multi-billion dollar business. Surely she was accustomed to speaking with an authoritative business voice. It just took Lucy by surprise. Her Hester was the eccentric, nerdy one.

Hester continued, "I mostly need your help in purchasing a home here. I'm planning on spending no more than five million euros on it." She scrunched up her face. "That isn't too little for you to work with me, is it?"

"Oh, no, no. Not at all."

Oliveto was nearly drooling at the prospect of working with one of the world's wealthiest people. Lucy could almost imagine him rubbing his hands together in greedy glee.

Lucy sat up. "Wine?"

Oliveto smiled. It was the smile the wolf made when the little pig built that house of twigs in his neighborhood.

"Yes, please."

Lucy poured his glass of wine, and as she did, she said, "There were just a couple of questions that came up on the background check that the Nilsson detectives would like answers for." She waved a hand back and forth, dismissively. "Don't worry, they are nothing. Just those little things that they like to nitpick."

Oliveto's jaw tensed.

Hester smiled at him. "You know, I really think they only came up because of this recent murder here in Venice. They somehow got the idea that you had known the victim." She shook her head and rolled her eyes. "I think she worked with you once upon a time, or something?"

Oliveto reddened. "Wait. Is this why you came to my office asking about that woman?" His suspicious eyes shifted back and forth from Lucy to Hester several times.

"I apologize for that," Hester said, the image of politeness. "One of the detectives had hoped I could simply clear it up before they issued their final report. But you didn't recall the name, so I told him that. But you know how these detectives can be. He wouldn't let it go." She shrugged apologetically.

He peered at Hester as if weighing the veracity of what she'd said.

Lucy took the baton. "If you can clear it up tonight, then we can report that to the detectives, and we can move forward with a contract with Hester. When we met with you the other day, we couldn't remember her maiden name. But we have that now. Aurelia Patela. What can you tell us about Signora Patela?"

Oliveto narrowed his eyes as if trying to recall such a person. Slowly, he began to nod.

"*Si, si*, I do remember her. We worked together many years ago though."

Lucy prepared to move into her assigned role as bad cop.

"At an import/export company?" she asked, all business now.

"Yes."

Lucy pulled out a legal pad and referred to her fake notes.

"You'll have to appreciate, Signor Oliveto, that with a company the size of Hester's we have in-house detectives who are exceptionally thorough. So some of these questions may sound odd, but you can trust that they have done their work. And I should tell you, we don't have the details on *how* they discovered the information that they did."

He took a long swallow of wine before giving the slightest of nods.

"All right, then, first, they want to hear about your relationship with Aurelia Patela's sister-in-law, Fausta Patela."

Lucy watched his reaction closely. He looked sincerely confused by the question.

"This Fausta person. I don't know anyone with that name."

Lucy pretended to check her notes.

"What about an Enzo Carotti?"

This time there was no missing the quiver of the jaw and brief widening of his eyes.

"Maybe that name sounds familiar. I think I did accounting for someone with that name. Maybe."

Again, Lucy made a pretense of referring to her notes. "The detectives had reason to suspect that you were taking care of selling a family heirloom for Carotti."

"Hmmm," he shook his head. "I don't recall that."

Lucy stared at him without blinking for several uncomfortable seconds. "We can come back to that." She made a note on the legal pad. As she did so, she could feel Oliveto's eyes on her.

"Signor Oliveto, what was your relationship with Aurelia Patela during the time you worked together?"

Lucy watched him swallow.

He shook his head. "She worked in the same department I worked in. Accounting. There was nothing more than that." Lucy knew he was fighting hard to maintain eye contact with her.

"There was never a personal relationship?"

He scowled. "No. Of course not."

Lucy graced him with another of her piercing stares.

"We will come back to that."

"Wait," he barked. "What does this have to do with my doing Signora Nilsson's accounting?"

"We must ascertain if the person with whom she will be doing financial transactions is at all susceptible to blackmail. You can certainly understand that we can't have such a person doing Hester's accounting here in Italy."

He eyed Lucy. "No one will ever blackmail me," he announced.

Hester, aka the good cop, said, "Of course not, Signor Oliveto. Remember, these detectives are ridiculously careful. We clearly have no concerns about you, or else the detectives would be here doing this interview themselves. This is just crossing T's and dotting I's." She gave him a dazzling smile.

Oliveto's jaw relaxed. His brow unknit itself. And he took a sip of wine.

"Good," he said. "I am no crook."

"Of course not," Hester said, waving away any such concern.

The moment Hester finished speaking, Lucy jumped back in.

"Back to Enzo Carotti. Were you aware that he was Aurelia's husband?"

His face grew dark. "I don't even know this man. How would I know who he married?"

Lucy ignored him. "Enzo Carotti never came to you talking about a painting, an old, masterpiece of a painting, that he wanted you to try to sell?"

He brought a hand down, hard, on the table.

"This is nonsense. I do not know what you are talking about."

Lucy tended to believe him. There was a touch of righteous anger in his tone.

"Fine. Let's return to Aurelia and the time you worked together." Lucy again referred to her notes, taking a moment to pretend she was searching for a particular notation.

"When was the last time you saw Aurelia Carotti?"

"I don't know. When she left the company? Twenty years ago?"

Now Lucy prepared to jump into the deep end without a life vest. "You didn't see her three months ago?"

He flinched. Lucy saw it.

"No."

Time to lie big. "You didn't start making payments to her once a month?"

He pushed his chair back and stood.

"I don't need your money this much," he growled at Hester.

"Sit down, Mr. Oliveto," Lucy directed him.

"Oh please," Hester implored him. "I do want you to be my accountant here. I think we would work together so well. Please just put up with these silly questions. I'm sure Lucy is almost finished."

Oliveto's face softened as he gazed at the beautiful woman begging him to work for her.

He sat back down.

Lucy said, "We know that you did, indeed, make these payments. Three payments, each for seven hundred and fifty euros." The lie tripped off her tongue. "There is nothing illegal or immoral about paying someone money. We just need to hear you tell us that you did make these payments. And why."

He flushed. Worked his jaw. Lucy forced herself to stay still and quiet. She maintained the uncomfortable eye contact.

"Okay. I did. I bought an antique table from a woman and made three payments. I did not know it was this Aurelia person I worked with so long ago. This woman looked very different."

Lucy fought off a triumphant grin. Her bluff had paid off.

She shot a look at Carrie and Oscar, and nodded once, almost imperceptibly. Oscar picked up his phone.

"Very well, I think that's all the information we need," Lucy said, a wide grin on her face. "Let's take a look at the menu, shall we?"

All of the tension in Oliveto's body seemed to disappear as Lucy handed him a menu. He took it with one hand while he raised his wine glass to his mouth with his other. In one huge gulp, he emptied the glass.

Pietro Affini and Maria Lazzara quietly sat down at Carrie and Oscar's table, their backs to Lucy and Hester, but close enough to hear everything. Affini was dressed sharply in a suit that probably had come from Milan, and Lazzara wore a soft peach suit. Neither looked like a police detective to Lucy's eye.

"You know, before we order," Lucy interrupted Oliveto's perusal of the menu, "there are a few things I think we still need to discuss."

"I cannot imagine what more," he grumbled as he slapped his menu down on the table.

Lucy smiled at him as he sneered at her. "If you don't want to continue with this that is fine. Hester Nilsson won't be your client, but of course, that is your choice, Signor Oliveto."

His eyes narrowed, and he thrust his jaw out. Lucy patiently waited him out. She glanced at Hester, who was gazing out on the canal, a coy smile on her lips.

He sighed noisily. "Fine. Let us do this thing. Get it over with." He turned his eyes to Hester, and with a smile that was plainly forced, he said, "I do want to…I do look forward to working with you, Signora Nilsson."

"Oh, excellent," Hester chirped.

Lucy once again made a pretense of referring to her 'detective's' notes.

"Signor Oliveto, our lead detective told us that Aurelia Carotti, née Patela, got pregnant during the time that you two worked together." Lucy saw him tense, so she hurried on before he could argue. "She had this baby, a boy, gave him up to adoptive parents who raised him. This boy recently turned eighteen and searched for his birth mother. He found her."

She paused to look at the notes as if to verify information, and Oliveto took the opportunity to say, "What does this have to do with me? Your *detectives* sound incompetent." His voice was low and threatening. Lucy saw Chief Inspector Affini turn his head slightly in the direction of her table.

"Aurelia's son found her in February. That was the same month you made your first payment to Aurelia. You made two more payments, one in March and one in April. Each time on the twentieth. If you were to have continued on the same payment schedule, your fourth payment would have been made seven days ago. But it never was."

Oliveto brought his fist down on the table, causing

Hester's untouched glass of wine to slosh over the rim.

"I told you," he began through clenched teeth, "that I bought a table from her. It cost the three payments. I was finished paying her for the table."

"But you must admit that the timing is quite suspicious," Lucy said.

"A mere coincidence."

Without answering his charge, she read her notes, and keeping her eyes cast down at them said, "They spoke to someone Aurelia knew at the time you two worked together. This person told them that Aurelia was miserable at her job. And the only name the person remembered her ever mentioning at the job was yours, Signore." She met his cold stare.

When he didn't say anything in answer, Lucy said, "The detective believes it is possible that you had an affair with Aurelia and she became pregnant. Then this past February she told you she would tell the boy about you, and when you in turn told her to keep you out of it, she began to blackmail you. But you—"

"This is *merda*!" This time he didn't bother to keep his voice down. Lucy could feel the eyes of nearby diners turn to her table.

She didn't need to ask Hester for a translation of the local expletive. She had a good sense of what it meant.

This time Affini didn't limit himself to a casual glance, but instead pushed his chair back and stood.

"Signor Oliveto, I suggest you keep your voice down," Affini directed the red-faced man.

"What's this? One of your detectives?"

Affini smiled. Lucy was impressed with how professional it looked. "No, I am one of Venice's detectives. Currently, in charge of the Aurelia Carotti murder case." His tone was calm, measured, unruffled.

All of the redness drained from Oliveto's face.

"I would like Signora Tuppence to continue with what she was saying," Affini said.

"Thank you, *Capo Ispettore* Affini," Lucy said. "We believe that you, Signor Oliveto, got tired of paying the blackmail and put a permanent end to the arrangement by killing Aurelia."

"That is ludicrous," he said coldly.

Lucy peered at him, moving her face closer to his. "You know, I've met Aurelia's son, and he has some of your features. Your nose. Your hair." She nodded.

Lucy turned her attention to Affini. "Here are the bullet points. First, Aurelia worked with Oliveto at the time she got pregnant. We know she had mentioned Oliveto's name to a friend of hers. The son showed up in February, the same month Oliveto made his first payment to Aurelia. The fourth payment wasn't made on the date expected. I believe he went to Burano to supposedly make the payment on the day Aurelia was killed. She met him near the boat dock at the end of the island, to get her money. He killed her, threw her in the canal."

Affini peered at Oliveto while he thought it through. "I see where the dots connect," he said, turning to Lucy. "But we don't have any evidence that puts him on the scene at the time." He cocked a brow in question.

"That's right! You don't," Oliveto, who'd been silent for some time, blurted out.

"But, maybe we do." Lucy reached into her purse and brought out a computer thumb drive. She handed it to Affini.

"This is footage my cameraman, Oscar, took on Burano at the time of the murder, or very soon after. There is an image of someone bending over the spot on the canal where Aurelia's body was found. This person doesn't act like someone who is shocked to find a body in the canal. No, he just moseys away from the spot. It isn't clear. You can't see the person's face clearly. But I think if your excellent forensic people work their magic on it you might be able to see the person's right hand."

Lucy reached over and pointed to Oliveto's ugly ring— the one on his right pinkie finger.

"I'm fairly certain you'll be able to see this ring in the picture."

One corner of Affini's mouth turned up in an impressed half-smile. "That would be helpful, yes."

"And of course with your resources, you'll be able to trace his movements that day. See if he took a boat to Burano, all of that. I think you'll find it all falls right into place."

Affini cocked his head at Maria Lazzara, who stood.

Oliveto, who just minutes earlier had been a bright shade of angry red, then a shocked white, was now taking on a green hue.

To Oliveto, he directed something in Italian or Venetian.

Lucy made out the word Questura. She assumed there was a boat ride in Oliveto's near future.

Everyone stood. Lucy shook Affini's hand, then Maria's.

To Oliveto, who stood with his hands locked in handcuffs behind his back, Lucy said, "By the way, I wouldn't count on doing any accounting work for Miss Nilsson." She gave him a mean-spirited wink as he was led away.

Not until she had watched the police detectives and Oliveto leave the restaurant did Lucy give herself a shake.

"Oh my," she said with a sigh. Hester and Carrie grinned at her.

"Well done!" Carrie gushed. "I don't know how you put all of that together. Paint me impressed."

"Truth be told, it could have gone a completely different way. If he hadn't admitted to making payments to Aurelia, I wouldn't have had anything."

"So what now?" Oscar asked.

"I don't know about you, but I'm going to sit down, have some wine, a good Italian seafood dinner, and relax."

Oscar smirked. "So eat, drink, and be merry?"

"Exactly," Lucy replied as she flopped back down into her chair.

Her three friends joined her at the table. As they pored over the menu, Oscar ordered another bottle of wine.

From below, the strains of music from a gondola in the canal reached Lucy's ears. An accordion and a male singer. She guessed it was a gondolier singing—he wasn't always in tune.

When they finished their sumptuous meal, she would treat everyone to a nighttime gondola ride on the Grand Canal.

La dolce vita.

~ twenty seven ~

WITH THE MORNING BELLS OF St. Mark's ringing in the distance, Lucy attempted to tame a rogue lock of hair.

She would have liked a day off from the travel business after the emotional exhaustion of the previous evening, but she had been able to convince Hester that the Accademia would be enough to accomplish for the day. There had originally been a second museum on the schedule as well.

She dressed for comfort—cream linen capris, and a loose denim shirt, along with sneakers. The heat had broken and the day was supposed to be pleasant.

Just before she was ready to leave her room, there was a soft knock on her door.

She opened it to find a grinning Hester, who stepped into the room without so much as a *permesso.*

Hester clapped her hands together. "I received a call from Caterina at the Accademia! She said they have the preliminary findings on the painting and that she'd meet with us today when we're there and share the results." Hester spoke so rapidly Lucy had difficulty following along.

"That's great," Lucy said, trying to sound excited, and hoping excitement was indeed the appropriate emotion for whatever Hester had just said.

Hester pranced in place. "You ready to go?" she squealed.

"I am. Are our in-front-of-camera talent and camera operator ready too?"

"Yes. They are. In the lobby."

Lucy smiled at her enthusiastic friend. She could understand that for an art history major the possible discovery of a long-lost masterpiece would be a once in a lifetime experience.

Hester was about to jump out of her skin, she was so excited.

"Then let's get going," Lucy said, with a wink.

Lucy and Hester stood in a cluttered workshop located in a wing at the back of the Accademia, waiting for Caterina. At the same time, Carrie and Oscar were setting up for the first shot of the day in a section of the museum with several paintings by Giovanni Bellini.

In the workshop, an art restorer worked on a painting under a large, but not overly bright, lamp. He wore glasses with magnifiers attached to the lenses and labored on an extraordinarily small spot using what looked like a sharp dental tool. In other areas in the workshop, easels were concealed by cloths—Lucy assumed the cloths covered works in the process of restoration. An armless statue stood in one corner awaiting whatever fine work was to be done on it.

The smell of paint and turpentine filled the air. Lucy mused on the fact that it wasn't an unpleasant smell, which surprised her.

Caterina swept into the room. She wore black slacks and a purple camisole all topped off with a filmy duster-length jacket that was decorated with swirls of color. It billowed behind her as she entered the workshop.

"Hester!" Caterina kissed her on both cheeks. When she was finished with Hester, she gave Lucy the same greeting.

"I had the painting brought in here so we could all admire it," Caterina said as she seemingly floated across the room to one of the easels covered with a cloth. Lucy and Hester followed behind.

With a touch of ceremony she lifted the cloth, exposing the painting that Hester and Lucy had last seen in Aurelia's bedroom.

Hester breathed out an "Oh my." A hand flew to her mouth.

"I'm sure it must look different in proper light and sitting at the correct height for viewing," Caterina said.

"Indeed," Hester agreed. Lucy examined her friend's face. She saw her fighting off tears.

"Has its authenticity been determined?" Hester asked.

Caterina's eyes never left the painting. "The tests we were able to run here do indicate that it is likely the Canaletto that has been missing since the war."

"Oh, my!" This time Hester's utterance was more of a squeal than a prayer.

"However…" Caterina said pointedly. Hester shifted her eyes from the painting to Caterina. "We need to send it to

Rome for more conclusive testing. Having said that though, I must tell you that I feel in my heart that it is indeed Canaletto's *Piazza Santa Margherita*. And it is in remarkably good condition considering everything it's been through."

Hester clasped her hands together and pressed them to her heart. With her mouth open, she gazed lovingly at the painting.

Lucy, appreciating the historical significance of the moment, took in the picture Canaletto had painted so long ago. But if she were to be honest, she didn't care for it very much. It wasn't as glorious as the one she'd seen in this museum depicting the Grand Canal with all of the boat traffic and interesting characters. This one had a much more dour feel about it. She assumed Canaletto had had good painting days and not so good painting days. Though she would be the first to admit she didn't know great art from lesser art.

They visited with Caterina for another quarter of an hour, with Hester wiping away the occasional tear. Then it was time to join their comrades in the room with the Bellinis.

In the end, Lucy had to tug on Hester's arm to pull her away from the object of her reverence.

Carrie, wearing a dress of black polka dots and large red roses on a white background, belted at the waist, and topped off with red-framed cat-eye glasses, spoke to the camera about the glories to be discovered in Venice's Gallerie dell' Accademia. Lucy smiled, recognizing the dress from the Venice boutique where she, herself, had shopped. In fact,

Lucy had bought a similar dress—very Audrey Hepburn—but in a pale blue with small white polka dots. She'd loved it because the full skirt with the belt at her waist made her waist look a good size or two smaller than it actually was.

Lucy jumped when her phone rang. Hurriedly pulling it out of her purse so as not to disturb the church-like atmosphere of the room, she glanced at the screen.

Maria Lazzara.

She whispered a hello as she sprinted out of the room and into a quiet corridor.

"I have much to report. Shall we meet somewhere?" Maria cut to the chase.

"I'm at the Accademia. Is there somewhere near here where we could meet? If that isn't too far for you?"

"No, that would be perfect because I have an appointment near the Accademia Bridge later. There is a cafe near the *museo*. If you were facing the entrance, it would be just to the right. Meet me there in thirty minutes."

Maria didn't wait for Lucy's response before ending the call.

When she reentered the room, Oscar and Carrie were no longer filming. She strode over to where they stood with Hester, who looked slightly uncomfortable.

"Maria from the Questura just called," Lucy said, keeping her voice down. "She has news. I'm meeting her right outside at a cafe across from here. Anyone care to join me?"

Hester and Carrie were immediately on board. Oscar took a few seconds to hem and haw before eventually buckling.

A moment of panic hit Lucy. What if she'd gotten it all wrong, and Alberti Oliveto was not the murderer? It was with a racing heart that she left the museum for her meeting with Deputy Inspector Lazzara.

Lucy's group was already seated at an outdoor table, espressos sitting in front of them, when Maria arrived. She dashed inside to order her espresso before joining them.

They made the polite greetings as Maria stirred a half a packet of sugar into her cup.

She grinned at Lucy. "Well, you will be happy to know that you had most of it right. I suppose we owe you a gratitude." Maria took a sip of the espresso. "At one o'clock this morning, Signor Oliveto confessed to the murder of Aurelia Carotti."

Lucy released the breath she'd been holding pretty much since Maria's phone call.

Maria continued. "Your film footage was most helpful. We did manage to get a fairly clear shot of his right hand, and there it was. The ring. After that, there wasn't much he could do but confess."

Oscar smiled with satisfaction. "Glad it helped."

Maria smiled back at him. "Honestly, it may have made all the difference."

Oscar sat back, his chest puffed up, a sly grin on his mouth.

Maria continued. "He said that in February Aurelia visited him at his office to tell him that eighteen years ago she had his son and gave him up to be adopted. He had not been happy to hear this news. He had no idea she'd been pregnant. It had been a short affair, and toward the end of our questioning he admitted she had not always been a willing participant."

Lucy, Hester, and Carrie all made faces and sounds of disgust. Oscar, too, frowned and looked ill.

"The son had just found her, and Aurelia met with Oliveto. She wondered if he would like to meet his son. He did not. She left. But the next day she came back demanding payment for keeping his identity secret from the boy. For three months he made the payments, but he said he couldn't afford to continue with them. He knew only one way to get out of the arrangement."

"Yeah…" Lucy grumbled. "Did they meet on Burano for the payments?"

"They did. He borrowed a friend's boat each time and went to Burano, met her right there at the dock near where her body was found. So on this last time, they did the same thing. He knew by this time that she was a lacemaker, so he figured it was appropriate that she die by lace. Brought the length of machine-made lace and with no one anywhere nearby, he quickly strangled her and dumped her in the canal. But the tide was changing, and the body moved. He was indeed watching the body when you shot that footage, Oscar."

"Good timing, I guess," he said, sounding a tad self-deprecating.

"I would say it was," Maria agreed.

"Maria," Lucy began. "I spoke with the art historian at

the Accademia this morning, and it's looking like the painting really is the missing Canaletto. More tests will be done in Rome, but it sounds like that's just to make doubly sure before any announcements are made. Will the police be looking into how Aurelia happened to have it? Because we've heard some family stories…"

"Yes, there's a separate investigation being conducted by a group that works on art thefts. They would probably appreciate hearing the family rumors if you don't mind one more visit to the Questura." She lifted one brow in question.

"No, no trouble."

Maria downed the last sip of her espresso and stood. "I have another appointment to get to. But on behalf of *Capo Ispettore* Affini and myself, we would like to extend our thanks." The group stood, and each shook Maria's hand.

"Enjoy the rest of your time in Venice," she said as she left the table.

They told her they intended to.

For a few minutes they sat silently lost in their own thoughts. Then Lucy turned her attention to Hester, and asked, "Do you remember what Aurelia's friend, Martina, said when we were talking? About how Aurelia had said something about how she had her dead *nona* to thank for getting her out of money trouble?"

Hester squinted at Lucy. "Yeah…And we decided she meant the painting her grandmother left the family. That she could sell it."

"Right. That's what we *thought at the time*." Lucy shook a finger. "What if it was her grandmother's example of blackmailing a man she'd been intimate with that Aurelia was applying to her own life?"

Hester's eyes widened. Carrie leaned in closer to Lucy. "Well…" Hester began. "She did end up blackmailing Oliveto. That might have been it."

"And the painting actually had nothing whatsoever to do with the case," Lucy added. She laughed softly. "It was just a lucky coincidence that the Canaletto was found." Lucy shook her head and laughed at the irony, and soon her friends joined in.

Hester sat up straight. "I can tell you this, though. This art historian is thrilled that the missing Canaletto was found!"

"Do you three think you can finish up here?" Lucy asked. "I have one more thing I need to take care of."

She didn't wait for replies, but got up and headed toward the Accademia Bridge.

Lucy and Giovanni sat on the same step in front of the opera house that they'd sat on the first time they talked.

She had just told him about the arrest that was made. It had been difficult to tell the already grieving young man that it was his biological father who had murdered his biological mother. But he appeared to take the news well. Lucy consoled herself that at least he had never met the man, and Oliveto hadn't known of his son's existence until very recently.

But when it came to the motive for the murder, she

couldn't bring herself to tell him the truth. She knew it would only further break his heart to know his birth mother was a blackmailer. Of course, he might see or hear it in the news, but by then he would have had some time to digest the news of the murderer's identity.

In an effort to console him, Lucy said, "Giovanni, right after Aurelia's death I was in her apartment. On her dresser, there was only one photograph. It was of a young boy." He'd been sitting staring down at the ground, but when he heard this, he sat up and peered at Lucy.

"Did you give Aurelia a picture of yourself taken when you were a boy?" She asked her question in a soft voice, a church voice.

He nodded.

"It looked like she treasured it. With pride of place. She obviously loved you very much."

He pressed his eyes with a thumb and forefinger.

"*Grazie* for telling me that. I am happy she…" He couldn't finish as he swallowed hard.

"Giovanni, I would love if you would stay in contact with me," Lucy said, peering into the boy's beautiful eyes when he finally opened them. She assumed they were Aurelia's eyes.

He looked away and used the toe of his shoe to pulverize an already extinguished cigarette on the step. "I like that also." He sat back up, draped an arm over her shoulders and gave a soft squeeze. "You have been so nice to me. *Grazie mille.*"

"Do you still have my card? It has my phone number,

and as long as I'm in Europe, I think you should be able to reach me. At least text me. We leave for Paris soon. But I will call you too. Let's make sure I have your number." She dug out a piece of paper and pen from her purse and had him write it down.

They stood up, and Lucy pulled Giovanni in for a hug.

As they prepared to go their separate ways, she gave him a huge smile and choked back some tears. At least Aurelia got to meet the son she'd given up.

Before she was murdered.

～ twenty eight ～

TWO EVENINGS LATER, LUCY STOOD in the hotel lobby, anxiously awaiting the arrival of Nicolo. He had the evening off, and they had plans to dance in the square.

She wore the full-skirted, A-line dress that was similar to the one Carrie had worn at the Accademia. Pale blue, with tiny white polka dots it made her feel like Audrey Hepburn. She especially appreciated that when she spun around the skirt moved gracefully around her. Perfect for dancing.

What she hadn't planned for, however, were the other three participants in the evening. Hester, Carrie, and Oscar were joining Lucy on her date. Carrie had decided she was going to go dancing, and then cajoled Hester and Oscar into accompanying her.

Lucy found it interesting that Hester and Oscar wore the same clothes that they'd worn on their previous evening of dancing in the *piazza*. She wondered if each had done so as a way of capturing whatever magic they had felt that night.

As she had suspected, Nicolo looked surprised when he

entered the lobby and saw three extra dance participants. But, being the gentleman that he was, the expression was fleeting and quickly replaced with an infectious smile.

"My friends," he greeted the group dramatically. "I am so happy to see you all embracing the joy that is Venice." Turning his attention to Hester and Carrie, he added, "While I may be dancing most of the evening with Lucy, I hope you will each save me a dance." He cocked a rakish brow.

Carrie giggled, and Lucy wanted to slap some sense into her.

Hester told him that she would love to dance once with him.

With all of the niceties taken care of, he stepped over to Lucy and placed a kiss on each cheek. "*Buonasera*, my dear," he whispered in her ear. "You look beautiful."

She graced him with a warm smile, and the small group began to make their way to the square.

Walking into the *piazza* this time, Lucy took the time to soak it all in. They would be moving on in a few days—Paris awaited—and she wasn't sure when she would see the magnificent basilica and its romantic square again. She wanted to take a mental snapshot of the sights, of the sounds, of the way it felt to stand under the stars and be a part of something so far removed from anything she had experienced in her previous life.

When Nicolo took her hand and pulled her close for

their first dance of the evening, she put that into the snapshot as well.

This time, she wasn't in charge of the entertainment for the rest of the group—she focused only on her own experience. And as Nicolo twirled her during the first dance and her skirt spun about her, she couldn't help but grin ear to ear.

It was between the third and fourth dances that Nicolo brought up the one thing Lucy had been hoping to avoid.

"You leave soon, no?"

"I do."

"Lucy, I know what you have been thinking of me. That I'm that man who woos the women who pass through Venice. How do you say? Love them and leave them?"

Lucy chuckled uncomfortably, and then said, "Well…perhaps I have. A little. But it didn't matter. I've been enjoying our time together for what it is."

His forehead furrowed. "And what is it that you think this time is?"

"A special moment in time. One that cannot last. As much as I may wish it to be so."

He peered into her eyes. "We shall see about that." He left the enigmatic comment hanging in the air as Carrie walked by and he called out her name.

"My Lucy, if you'll excuse me," he said before lifting her hand and kissing it.

She watched as Nicolo and Carrie began to dance. Carrie was an excellent dancer, and the two looked good together.

Then her eye found Hester and Oscar. They walked

toward Lucy, standing so close together that their hands occasionally touched, though they were not holding hands.

"I'll go get us something to drink," Oscar told Hester.

When he was out of earshot, Lucy smiled at her friend, and asked, "Nice evening?"

"Very."

"Hester, I want to thank you. For everything. For this job. This adventure. This once-in-a-lifetime experience. You're a dear friend for doing this for me, for Carrie, for Oscar. Thank you!"

Hester smiled slyly. "As long as you don't think I'm going to supply a murder for you to solve at every one of our stops," she chided.

Both women laughed.

They linked arms and made their way over to the table where Oscar sat with a bottle of Pellegrino and a bottle of wine.

Hester sat down, but Lucy stood back a bit, taking one more mental snapshot of the magnificent Venice night.

～ the painting ～

While there actually is a painting, *Piazza Santa Margherita,* by Canaletto that was stolen by the Nazis, it sadly remains missing and is considered one of the world's top ten missing art masterpieces.

～ about the author ～

Monica Knightley is the author of mysteries, paranormal romances, and young adult novels. She makes her home in Portland, Oregon where the frequent rainy days are perfect for curling up with a good book and a hot cup of tea. When not fueling her reading addiction or writing her next book, Monica loves to travel, a passion that has led to *The Lucy Tuppence Mysteries*. She's thankful for a husband who loves traveling as much as she does.

You can visit Monica and find out about the latest additions to *The Lucy Tuppence Mysteries* and the *Stratford Upon Avondale* mystery series by going to:

http://www.monicaknightley.com/ *This is also where you can sign up for my Readers Group newsletter and be among the first to hear about new releases and giveaways! Occasionally I'll send out bonus materials and special recipes from Lucy's travels or from Stratford's tea room. I'll never share your information with any third party.*

https://www.facebook.com/monicaknightleyauthor

CPSIA information can be obtained
at www.ICGtesting.com
Printed in the USA
BVHW071019020520
579069BV00001B/239